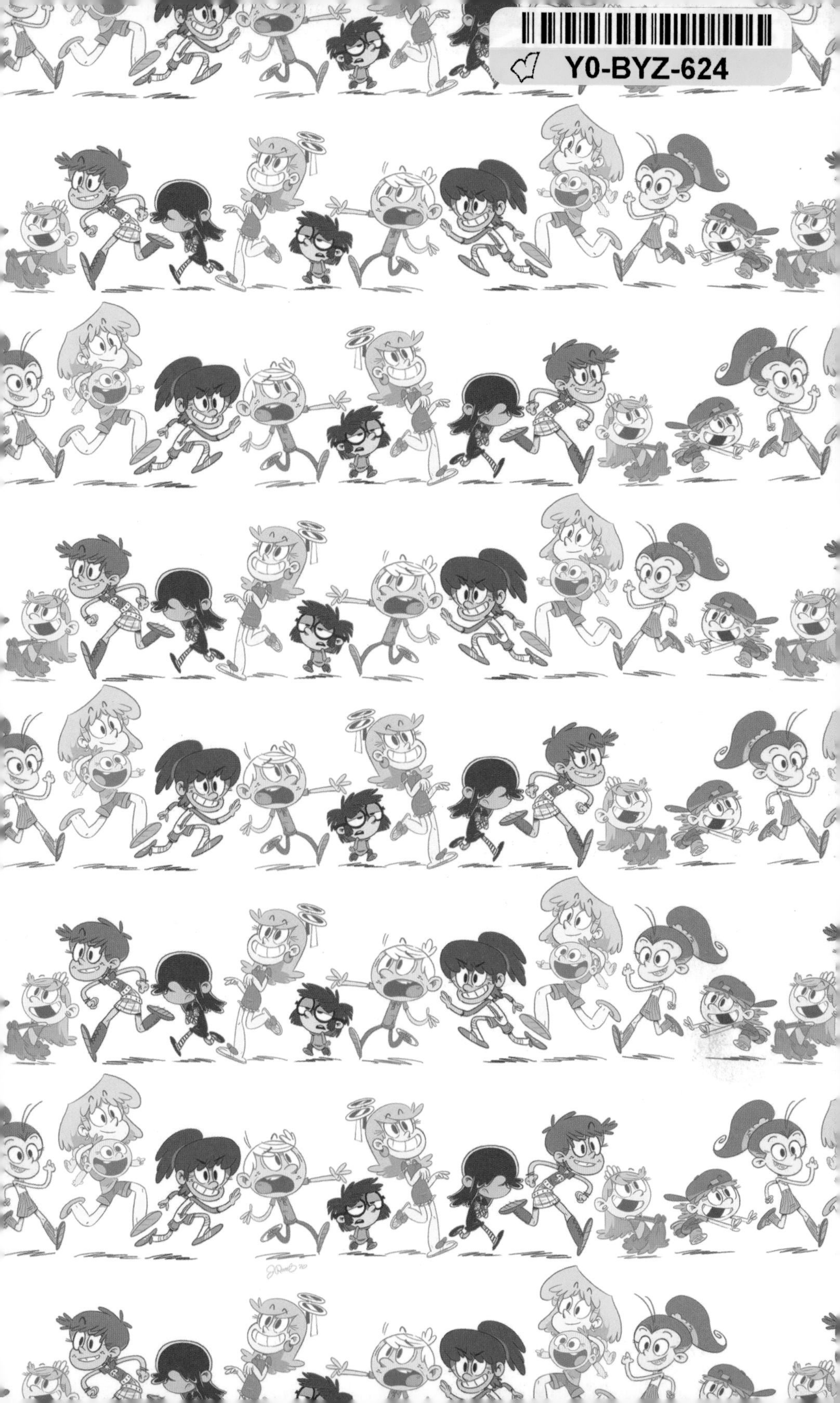

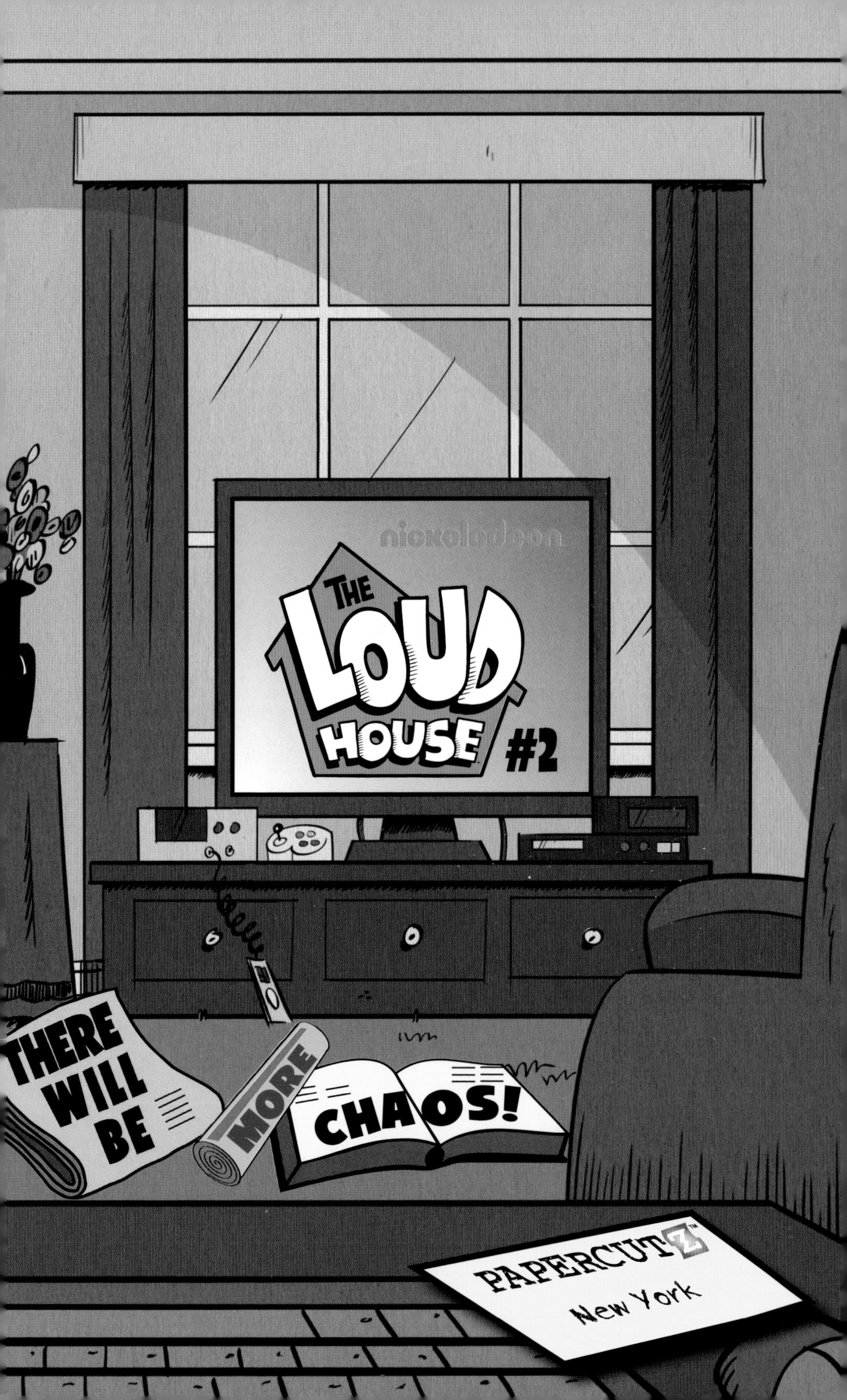
nickelodeon
THE LOUD HOUSE
#2
THERE WILL BE
MORE
CHAOS!
PAPERCUTZ
New York

nickelodeon GRAPHIC NOVELS AVAILABLE FROM PAPERCUTZ

THESE ALSO INCLUDE LOUD HOUSE STORIES!

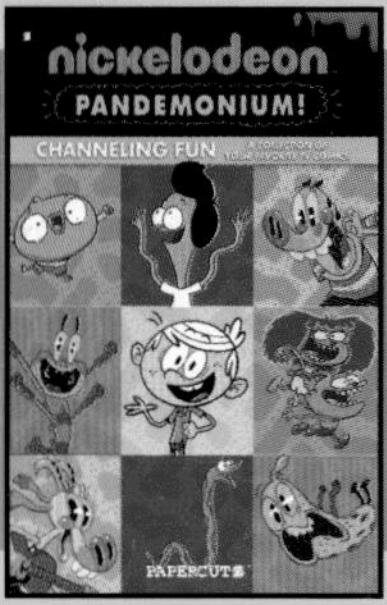
nickelodeon
PANDEMONIUM!
CHANNELING FUN
PAPERCUTZ

NICKELODEON PANDEMONIUM
#1
"Channeling Fun"

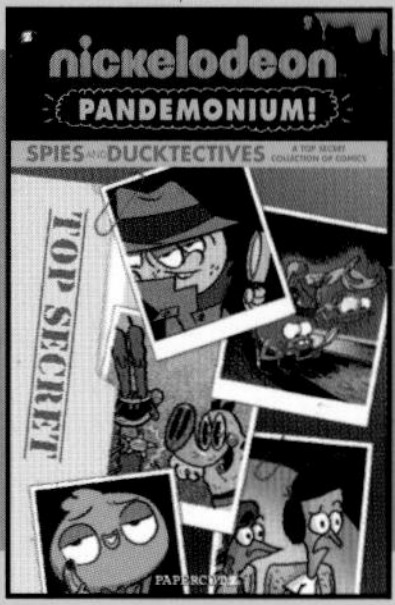
nickelodeon
PANDEMONIUM!
SPIES AND DUCKTECTIVES
TOP SECRET
PAPERCUTZ

NICKELODEON PANDEMONIUM
#2
"Spies and Ducktectives"

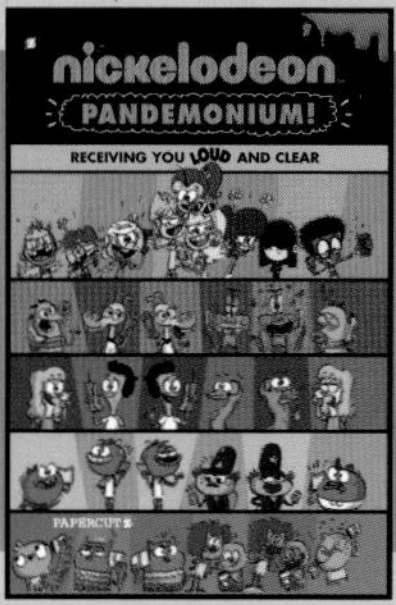
nickelodeon
PANDEMONIUM!
RECEIVING YOU LOUD AND CLEAR
PAPERCUTZ

NICKELODEON PANDEMONIUM
#3
"Receiving You Loud and Clear"

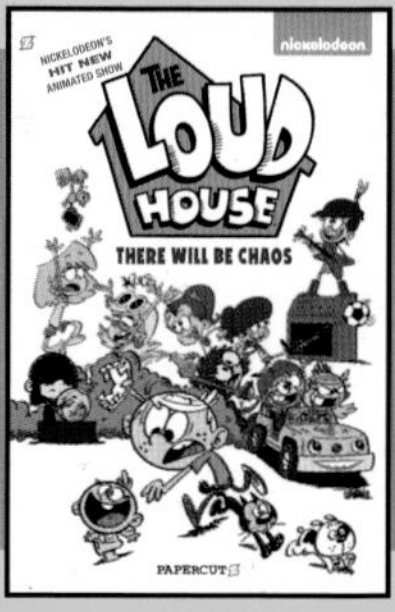
NICKELODEON'S HIT NEW ANIMATED SHOW
nickelodeon
THE LOUD HOUSE
THERE WILL BE CHAOS
PAPERCUTZ

THE LOUD HOUSE
#1
"There Will Be Chaos"

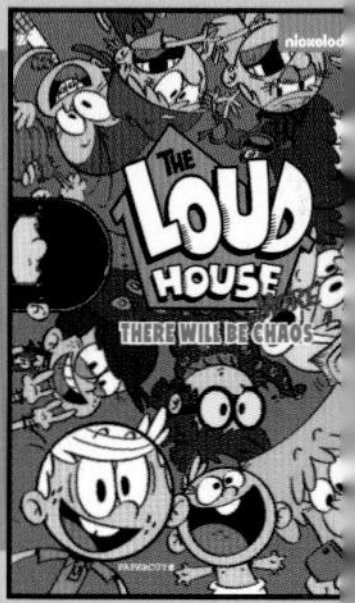
THE LOUD HOUSE
THERE WILL BE CHAOS
PAPERCUTZ

THE LOUD HOUSE
#2
"There Will Be More Chaos"

COMING SOON!

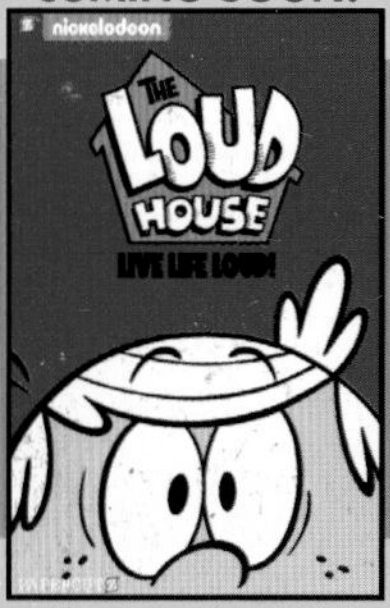
nickelodeon
THE LOUD HOUSE
LIVE LIFE LOUD!
PAPERCUTZ

THE LOUD HOUSE
#3
"Live Life Loud!"

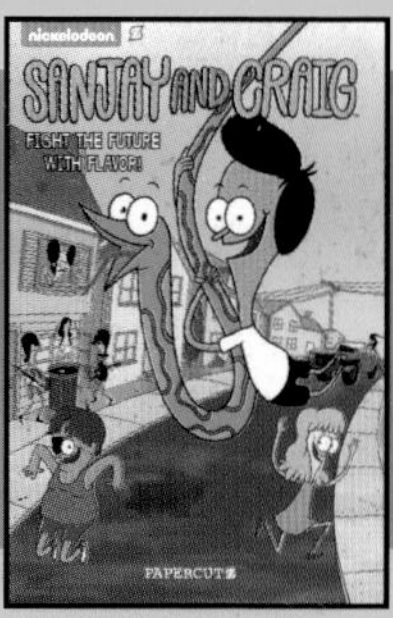
nickelodeon
SANJAY AND CRAIG
FIGHT THE FUTURE WITH FLAVOR!
PAPERCUTZ

SANJAY AND CRAIG
#1
"Fight the Future with Flavor"

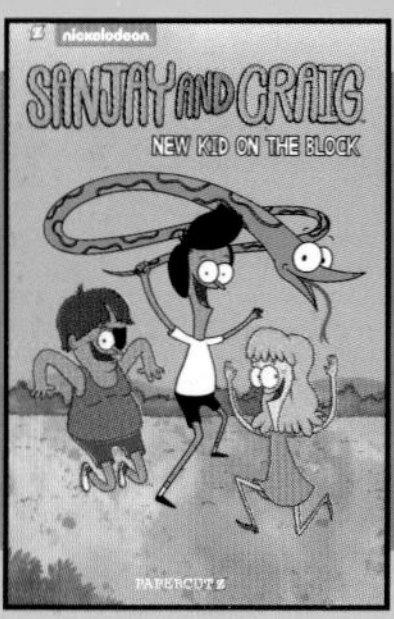
nickelodeon
SANJAY AND CRAIG
NEW KID ON THE BLOCK
PAPERCUTZ

SANJAY AND CRAIG
#2
"New Kid on the Block"

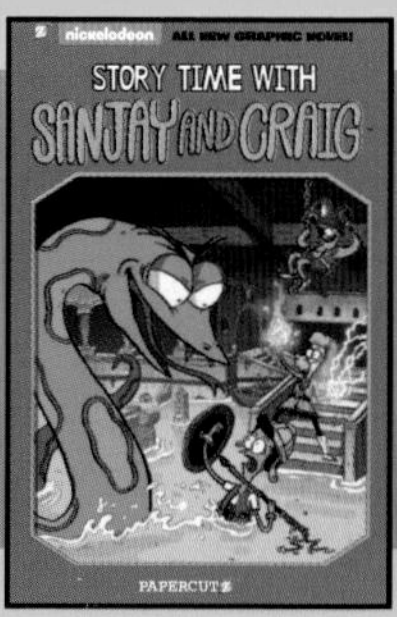
nickelodeon
STORY TIME WITH
SANJAY AND CRAIG
PAPERCUTZ

SANJAY AND CRAIG
#3
"Story Time with Sanjay and Craig"

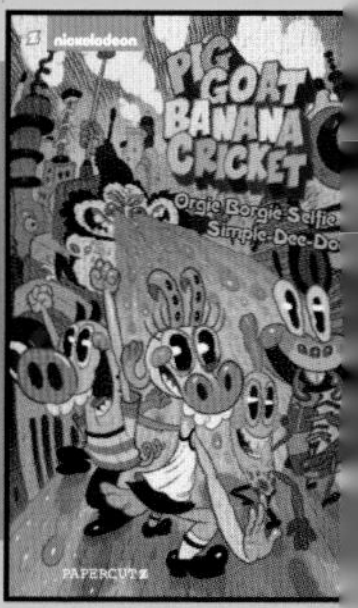
nickelodeon
PIG GOAT BANANA CRICKET
PAPERCUTZ

PIG GOAT BANANA CRICKET
#1
"Orgle Borgle Selfie Simple-Dee Doo!"

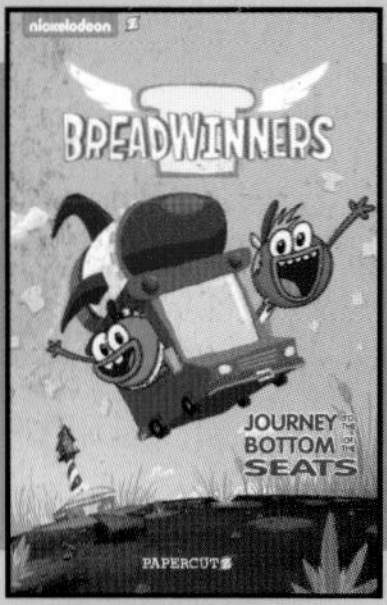
nickelodeon
BREADWINNERS
JOURNEY TO THE BOTTOM OF THE SEATS
PAPERCUTZ

BREADWINNERS
#1
"Journey to the Bottom of the Seats"

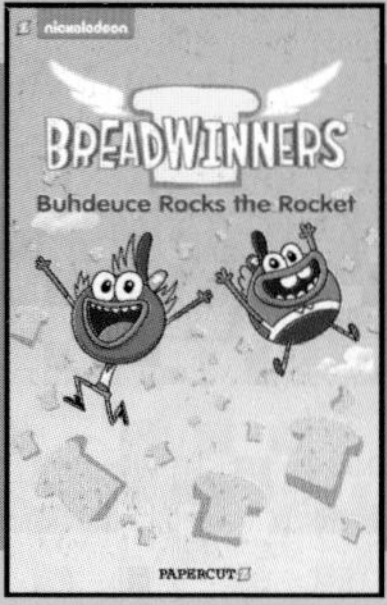
nickelodeon
BREADWINNERS
Buhdeuce Rocks the Rocket
PAPERCUTZ

BREADWINNERS
#2
"Buhdeuce Rocks the Rocket"

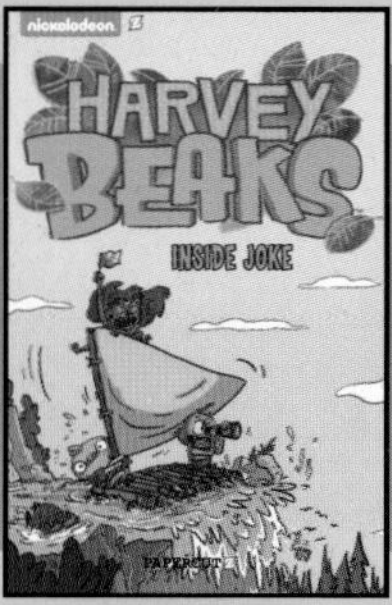
nickelodeon
HARVEY BEAKS
INSIDE JOKE
PAPERCUTZ

HARVEY BEAKS
#1
"Inside Joke"

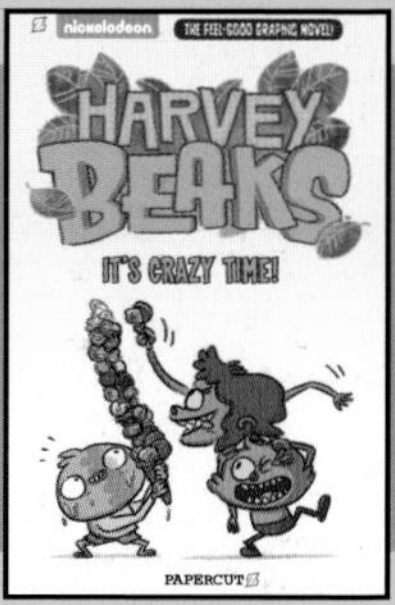
nickelodeon
THE FEEL-GOOD GRAPHIC NOVEL!
HARVEY BEAKS
IT'S CRAZY TIME!
PAPERCUTZ

HARVEY BEAKS
#2
"It's Crazy Time"

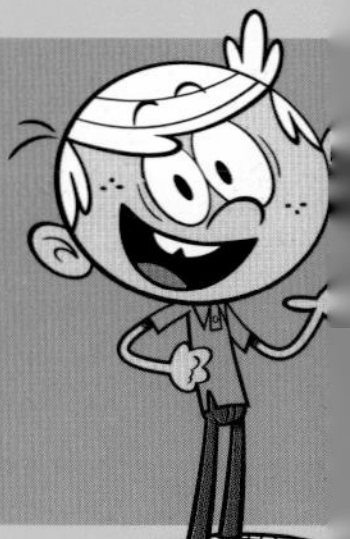

Nickelodeon graphic novels are available for $7.99 each in paperback, $12.99 each in hardcover. NICKELODEON PANDEMINIUM #3 is $8.99 each in paperback, $13.99 each in hardcover. Available from booksellers everywhere. You can also order online from Papercutz.com, or call 1-800-886-1223, Monday through Friday, 9-5 EST. MC, Visa, and AmEx accepted. To order by mail, please add $5.00 for postage and handling for the first book ordered, $1.00 for each additional book and make check payable to NBM Publishing. Send to: Papercutz, 160 Broadway, Suite 700, East Wing, New York, NY 10038.

Nickelodeon Graphic Novels are also available digitally wherever e-books are sold.

THERE WILL BE MORE CHAOS

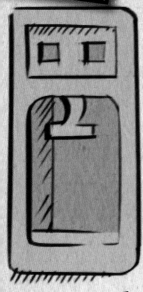

Meet the Loud Family
5

Watch Out for Papercutz
59

nickelodeon THE LOUD HOUSE #2 "THERE WILL BE MORE CHAOS

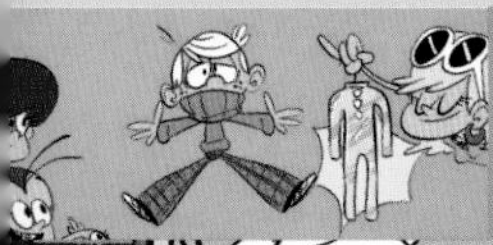

"BACK TO SCHOOL SHOPPING"
Sammie Crowley & Whitney Wetta—Writers
Erin Hyde—Artist, Colorist, Letterer

"TIRED OUT"
Kevin Sullivan—Writer
Ari Castleton—Artist , Letterer
Diem Doan—Colorist

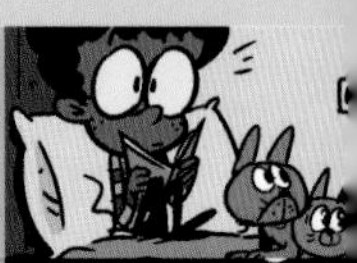

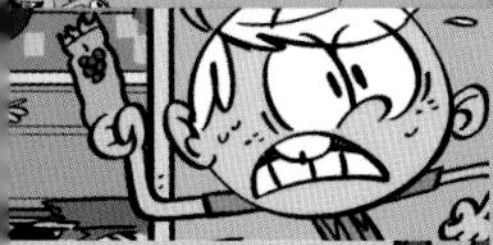

"POPSICLE PROBLEMS"
Kevin Sullivan—Writer
Diem Doan—Artist , Letterer
Amanda Rynda—Colorist

"LIGHTS OUT"
Jordan Koch
Writer, Artist, Letterer, Colorist

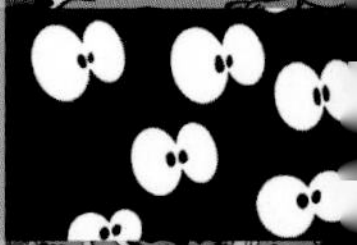

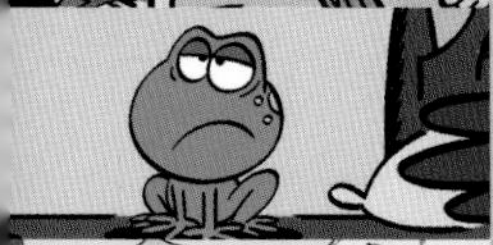

"HOPPILY EVER AFTER"
Jordan Koch
Writer, Artist, Letterer, Colorist

"THE 10–HEADED BEAST"
Jared Morgan
Writer, Artist, Letterer, Colorist

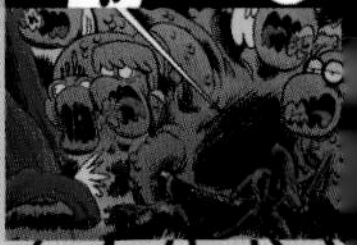

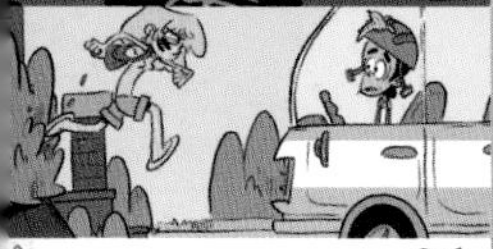

"DATE NIGHT"
Sammie Crowley & Whitney Wetta—Writers
Ida Hem—Artist, Colorist, Letterer

"TRAFFIC JAM"
Jordan Koch—Writer
Diem Doan—Artist, Letterer, Colorist

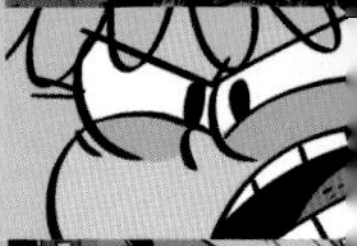

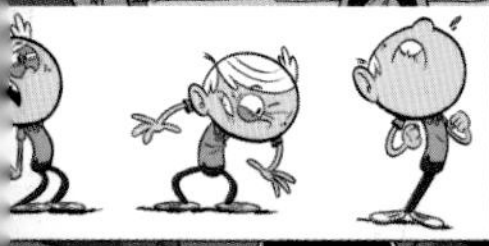

"THE SNEEZE!"
Jared Morgan
Writer, Artist, Letterer, Colorist

"BAGGED AND BOARDED"
Jared Morgan
Writer, Artist, Letterer, Colorist

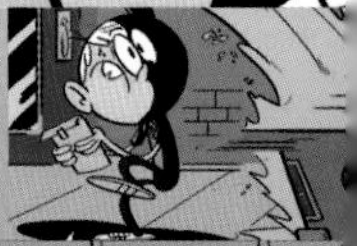

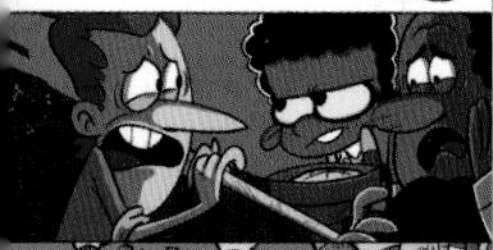

"CLYDE'S CAT-ASTROPHE"
Kevin Sullivan—Writer
Ida Hem—Artist, Colorist, Letterer

"SHOE STYLIN'"
Sammie Crowley & Whitney Wetta—Writers
Adam Reed—Artist, Colorist, Letterer

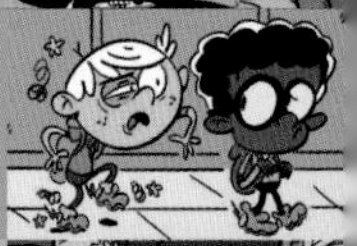

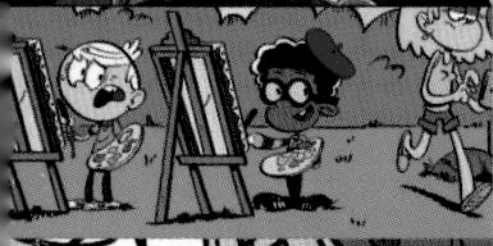

"LAND ESCAPE"
Jared Morgan
Writer, Artist, Letterer, Colorist

"THE ART OF COOKING"
Jared Morgan
Writer, Artist, Letterer, Colorist

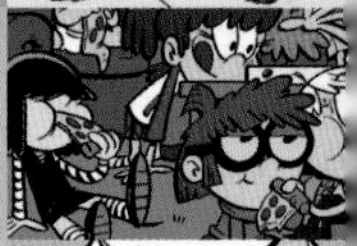

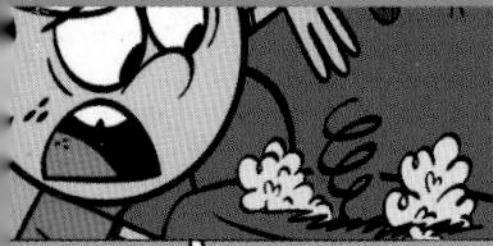

"HOUSE TRAINING"
Jordan Koch
Writer, Artist, Letterer, Colorist

"THE BORROWERS"
Sammie Crowley & Whitney Wetta—Writers
Agny Innocente—Artist, Letterer
Amanda Rynda—Colorist

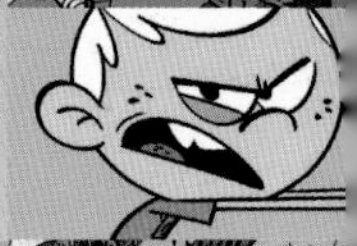

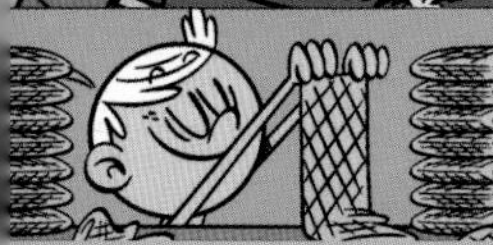

"TROPICAL PARADISE"
Jordan Koch
Writer, Artist, Letterer, Colorist

"MUSCLE FISH"
Miguel Puga—Writer, Artist, Letterer
Diem Doan—Colorist

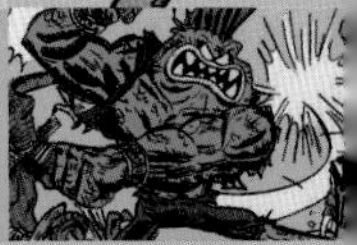

CHRIS SAVINO – Cover Artist
JAMES SALERNO – Sr. Art Director/Nickelodeon
SEAN GANTKA–Speial Thanks
DAWN GUZZO – Design
JEFF WHITMAN – Editor
JOAN HILTY – Comics Editor/Nickelodeon
JIM SALICRUP
Editor-in-Chief

ISBN: 978-1-62991-824-2 paperback edition
ISBN: 978-1-62991-825-9 hardcover edition

Printed in China
November 2017

Distributed by Macmillan
First Printing

MEET THE LOUD FAMILY

and friends!

LINCOLN LOUD
THE MIDDLE CHILD (11)

At 11 years old, Lincoln is the middle child, with five older sisters and five younger sisters. He has learned that surviving the Loud household means staying a step ahead. He's the man with a plan, always coming up with a way to get what he wants or deal with a problem, even if things inevitably go wrong. Being the only boy comes with some perks. Lincoln gets his own room – even if it's just a converted linen closet. On the other hand, being the only boy also means he sometimes gets a little too much attention from his sisters. They mother him, tease him, and use him as the occasional lab rat or fashion show participant. Lincoln's sisters may drive him crazy, but he loves them and is always willing to help out if they need him.

ENI LOUD
HE FASHIONISTA (16)

Leni is the ditsiest of the Loud sisters. She spends most of her time designing outfits and accessorizing (though she probably can't spell the word). She is easily distracted by shiny objects, always falls for Luan's pranks, and sometimes walks into walls when she's talking (she's not great at doing two things at once). Leni might be flighty, but she's the sweetest of the Loud siblings and truly has a heart of gold (even though she's pretty sure it's a heart of blood).

LORI LOUD
THE OLDEST (17)

As the first-born child of the Loud clan, Lori sees herself as the boss of all her siblings. She feels she's paved the way for them and deserves extra respect. Her signature traits are rolling her eyes, texting her boyfriend Bobby, and literally saying "literally" all the time. Because she's the oldest and most experienced sibling, Lori can be a great ally, so it pays to stay on her good side.

LUNA LOUD
THE ROCK STAR (15)

Luna is loud, boisterous and freewheeling, and her energy is always cranked to 11. She thinks about music so much that she even talks in song lyrics. On the off-chance she doesn't have her guitar with her, everything can and will be turned into a musical instrument. You can always count on Luna to help out, and she'll do most anything you ask, as long as you're okay with her supplying a rocking guitar accompaniment.

LUAN LOUD
THE JOKESTER (14)

Luan's a standup comedienne who provides a nonstop barrage of silly puns. She's big on prop comedy too – squirting flowers and whoopee cushions – so you have to be on your toes whenever she's around. She loves to pull pranks and is a really good ventriloquist – she is often found doing bits with her dummy, Mr. Coconuts. Luan never lets anything get her down; to her, laughter IS the best medicine.

LYNN LOUD
THE ATHLETE (13)

Lynn is athletic and full of energy and is always looking for a teammate. With her, it's all sports all the time. She'll turn anything into a sport. Putting away eggs? Jump shot! Score! Cleaning up the eggs? Slap shot! Score! Lynn is very competitive, tends to be superstitious about her teams, and accepts almost any dare.

LUCY LOUD
THE EMO (8)

You can always count on Lucy to give the morbid point of view in any given situation. She is obsessed with all things spooky and dark – funerals, vampires, séances, and the like. She wears mostly black and writes moody poetry. She's usually quiet and keeps to herself. Lucy has a way of mysteriously appearing out of nowhere, and try as they might, her siblings never get used to this.

LANA LOUD
THE TOMBOY (6)

Lana is the rough-and-tumble sparkplug counterpart to her twin sister, Lola. She's all about reptiles, mud pies, and muffler repair. She's the resident Ms. Fix-it and is always ready to lend a hand – the dirtier the job, the better. Need your toilet unclogged? Snake fed? Back-zit popped? Lana's your gal. All she asks in return is a little A-B-C gum, a handful of kibble (she often sneaks it from the dog bowl).

LOLA LOUD
THE BEAUTY QUEEN (6)

Lola could not be more different from her twin sister, Lana. She's a pageant powerhouse whose interests include glitter, photo shoots, and her own beautiful, beautiful face. But don't let her cute, gap-toothed smile fool you; underneath all the sugar and spice lurks a Machiavellian mastermind. Whatever Lola wants, Lola gets – or else. She's the eyes and ears of the household and never resists an opportunity to tattle on trouble-makers. But if you stay on Lola's good side, you've got yourself a fierce ally – and a lifetime supply of free makeovers.

LISA LOUD
THE GENIUS (4)

Lisa is smarter than the rest of her siblings combined. She'll most likely be a rocket scientist, or a brain surgeon, or an evil genius who takes over the world. Lisa spends most of her time working in her lab (the family has gotten used to the explosions), and says her research leaves little time for frivolous human pursuits like "playing" or "getting haircuts." That said, she's always there to help with a homework question, or to explain why the sky is blue, or to point out the structural flaws in someone's pillow fort. Lisa says it's the least she can do for her favorite test subjects, er, siblings.

LILY LOUD
THE BABY (15 MONTHS)

Lily is a giggly, drooly, diaper-ditching free spirit, affectionately known as "the poop machine." You can't keep a nappy on this kid – she's like a teething Houdini. But even when Lily's running wild, dropping rancid diaper bombs, or drooling all over the remote, she always brings a smile to everyone's face (and a clothespin to their nose). Lily is everyone's favorite little buddy, and the whole family loves her unconditionally.

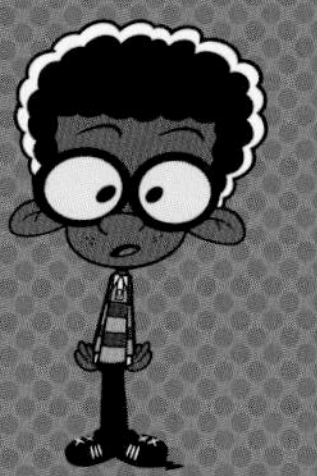

ƖYDE McBRIDE
Ξ BEST FRIEND (11)

ʏde is Lincoln's partner in me. He's always willing to along with Lincoln's crazy ıemes (even if he sees the ws in them up front). Lincoln d Clyde are two peas in a pod d share pretty much all of the me tastes in movies, comics, shows, toys – you name it. an only child, Clyde envies coln – how cool would it be to ways have siblings around to k to? But since Clyde spends much time at the Loud house- ld, he's almost an honorary ling anyway. He also has a ıjor crush on Lori.

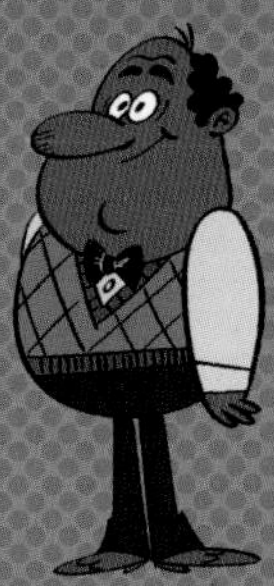

HAROLD McBRIDE
CLYDE'S DAD

Harold, one of Clyde's Dads, is a level-headed straight-shooter with a heart of gold. The more easygo-ing of Clyde's dads, Harold often has to convince Howard that it's okay for them to not constantly hover over Clyde. Harold also has an athletic side – he played baseball in college and he and Howard are always up for challenging themselves physically, going as far as to take part in the Royal Woods Samurai Warrior competition.

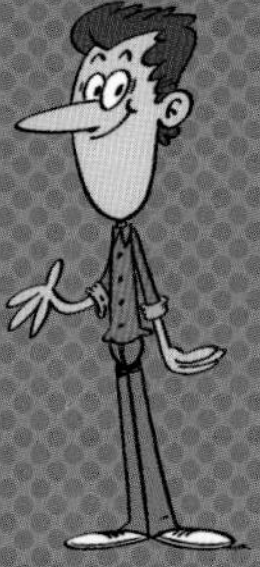

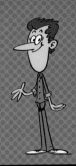

HOWARD McBRIDE
CLYDE'S OTHER DAD

Howard, Clyde's other Dad, is a constantly anxious helicopter parent. Howard is emotional, whether it be sad times (like when Clyde stubbed his toe) or happy (like when Clyde and Lincoln beat that really tough video game). Howard is end-lessly supportive of Clyde and is always by his side (watching to make sure nothing goes wrong). When he's not watching Clyde's every move, he's taking care of the McBrides' cats, Cleopawtra and Nepurrtiti or playing the jazz saxophone.

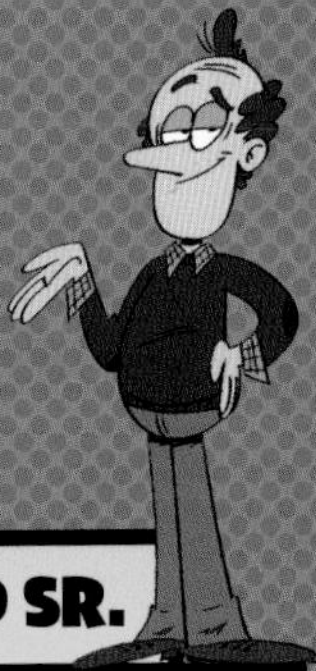

ƳNN LOUD SR.

Dad (Lynn Loud Sr.) is a fun- oving, upbeat aspiring chef. A kid-at-heart, he's not above aking part in the kids' zany chemes. In addition to cooking, Dad loves his van, playing he cowbell and making puns. Before meeting Mom, Dad pent a semester in England and ıas been obsessed with British culture ever since – and some- imes "accidentally" slips into a British accent. When Dad's ıot wrangling the kids, he's pursuing his dream of opening ıis own restaurant where he ıopes to make his "Lynn-sagnas" world famous.

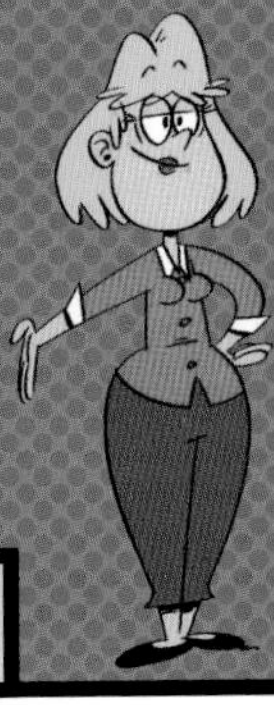

RITA LOUD

Mother to the eleven Loud kids, Mom (Rita Loud) wears many different hats. She's a chauffeur, homework-checker and barf-cleaner-upper all rolled into one. She's always there for her kids and ready to jump into action during a crisis, whether it's a fight between the twins or Leni's missing shoe. When she's not chasing the kids around or at her day job as a dental hygienist, Mom pursues her passion: writing. She also loves taking on house projects and is very handy with tools (guess that's where Lana gets it from). Between writing, working and being a mom, her days are always hectic but she wouldn't have it any other way.

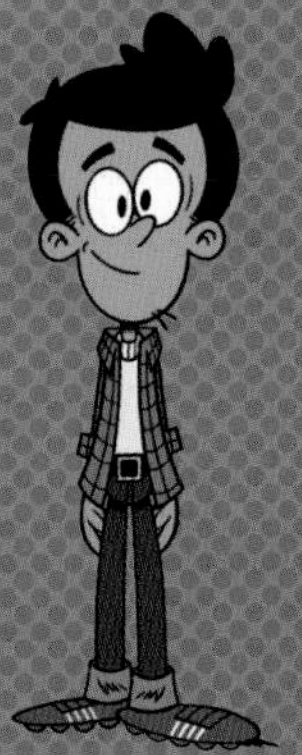

BOBBY SANTIAGO
LORI'S BOYFRIEND (17)

Bobby is sweet, a little dense, and just as obsessed with Lori as she is with him. He's a romantic who considers each new week with Lori an anniversary worth celebrating. He's on the phone with her constantly and will do anything for her. He's a man of many jobs, including but not lim-ited to pizza delivery boy, pool lifeguard, mall security guard, and grocery stock boy.

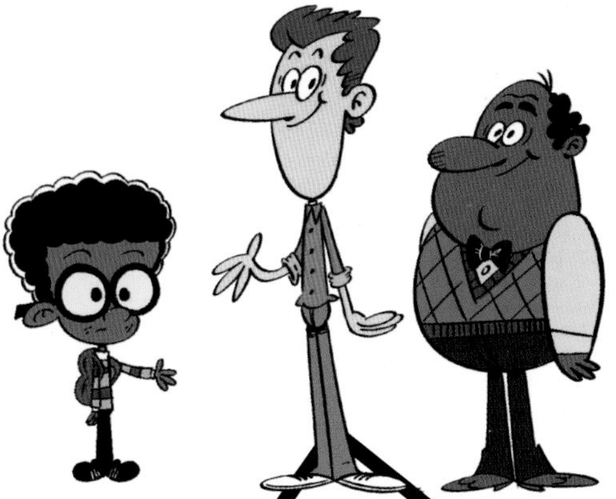

INTRODUCTION

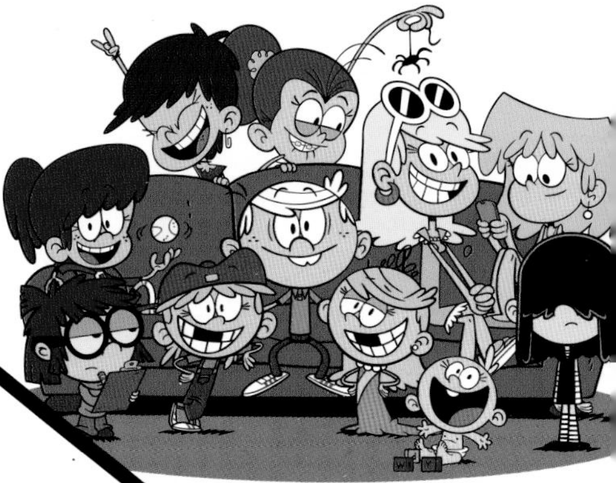

What is family?

Growing up as number 9 of 10 kids — to me, that was family.

My best friend had only one sibling. That was family to him.

Families come in all shapes and sizes and are more diverse today than ever before. My kids have friends who have two dads, friends who have two moms. Some friends have only one mom or one dad. Some friends live with their grandparents and some are blended by race and even religion. All of these are families and like with all families, there are good times and bad times and everything in between.

I hope to convey it all and represent it all in *THE LOUD HOUSE*. And if you watch the show or read these comics, I hope you see that *THE LOUD HOUSE* is about fun, *THE LOUD HOUSE* is about love, *THE LOUD HOUSE* is about acceptance, but most importantly, *THE LOUD HOUSE* is about family.

Enjoy!
Chris Savino
Creator of The Loud House

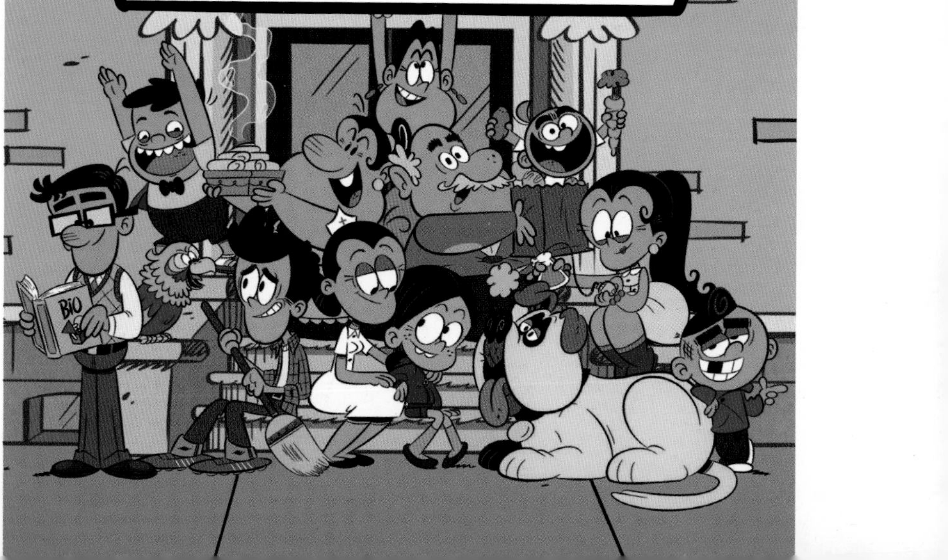
BiO

"BACK TO SCHOOL SHOPPING"

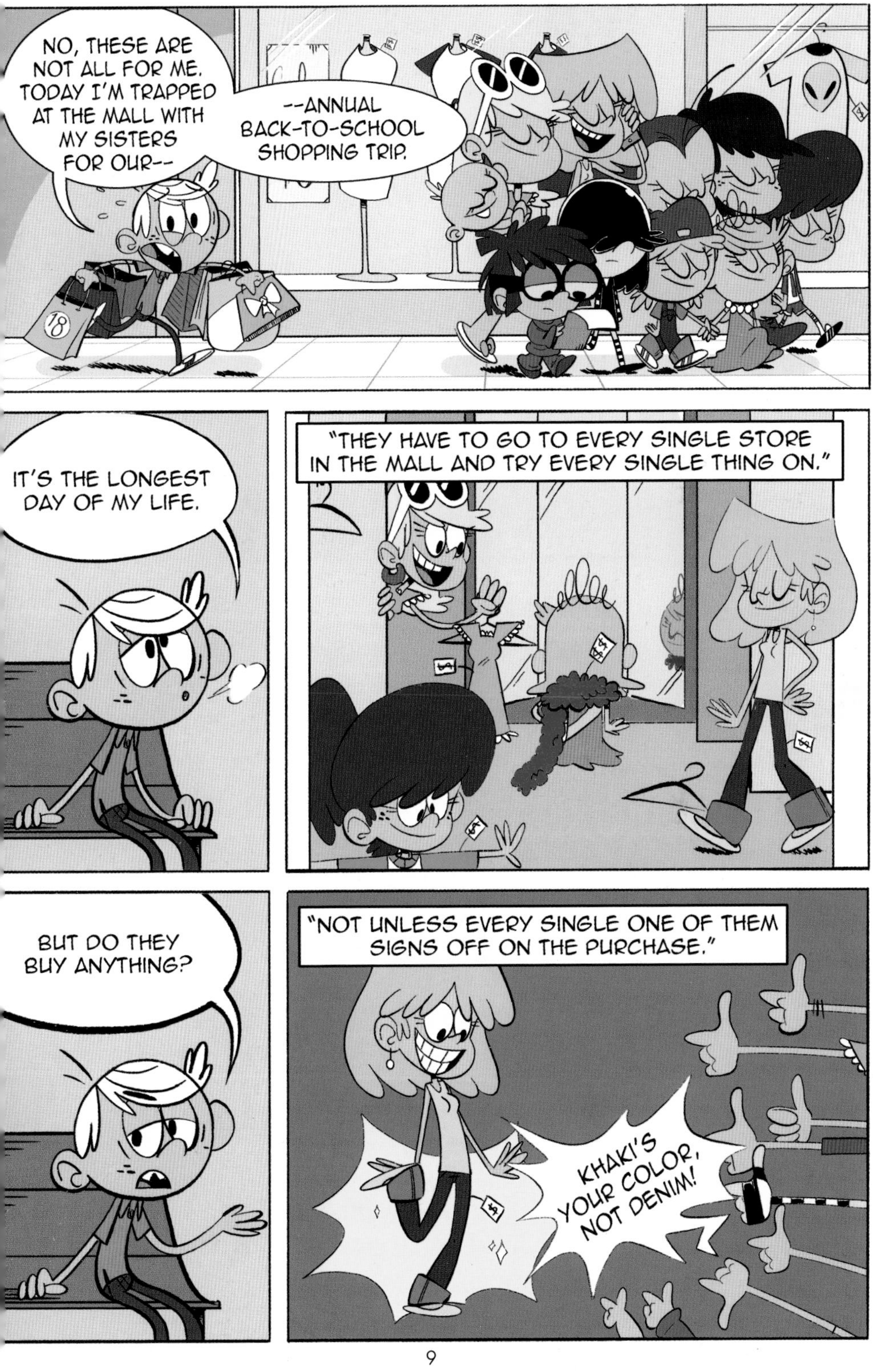

NO, THESE ARE NOT ALL FOR ME. TODAY I'M TRAPPED AT THE MALL WITH MY SISTERS FOR OUR--
--ANNUAL BACK-TO-SCHOOL SHOPPING TRIP.
IT'S THE LONGEST DAY OF MY LIFE.
"THEY HAVE TO GO TO EVERY SINGLE STORE IN THE MALL AND TRY EVERY SINGLE THING ON."
BUT DO THEY BUY ANYTHING?
"NOT UNLESS EVERY SINGLE ONE OF THEM SIGNS OFF ON THE PURCHASE."
KHAKI'S YOUR COLOR, NOT DENIM!

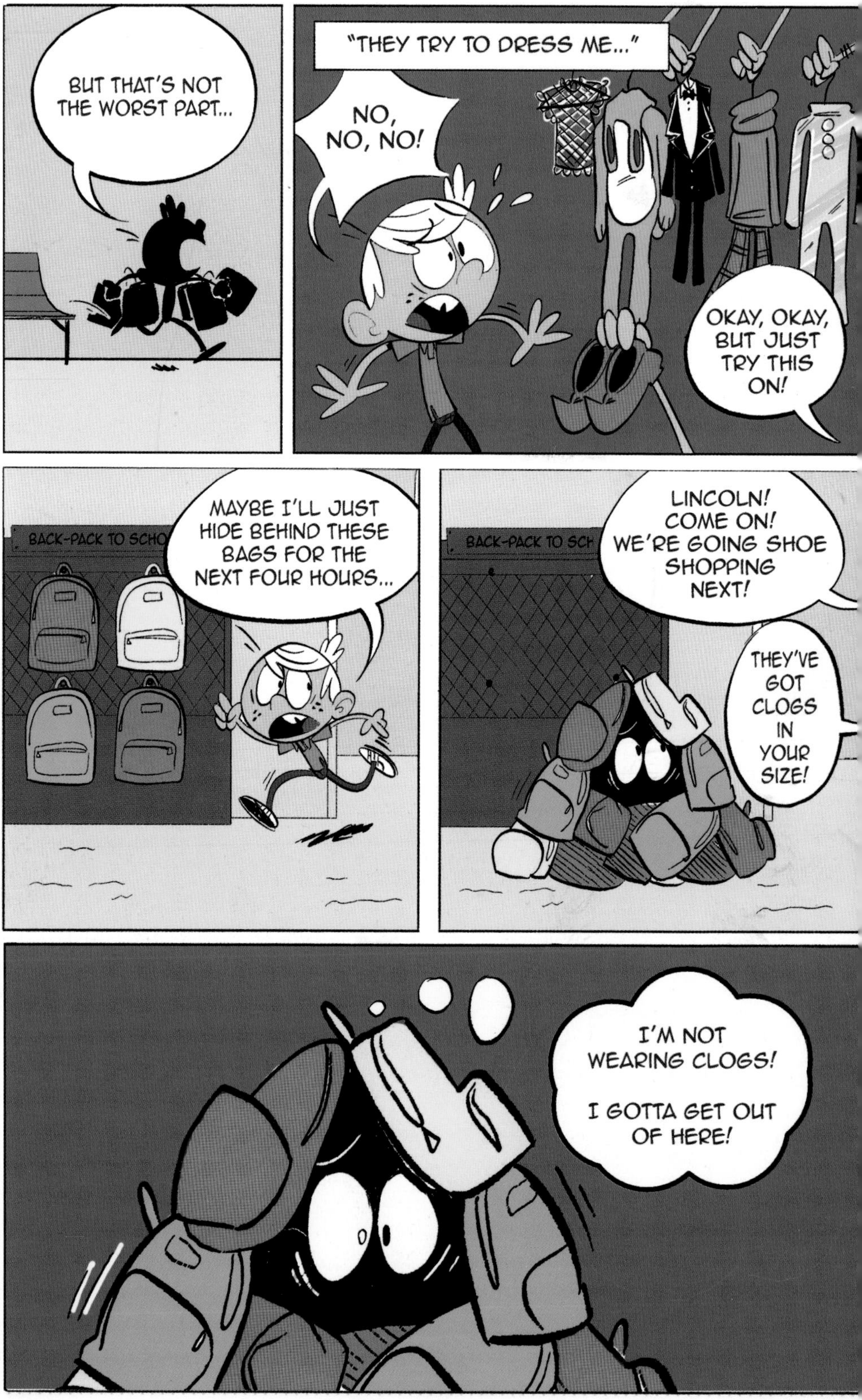
BUT THAT'S NOT THE WORST PART...
"THEY TRY TO DRESS ME..."
NO, NO, NO!
OKAY, OKAY, BUT JUST TRY THIS ON!
BACK-PACK TO SCHO
MAYBE I'LL JUST HIDE BEHIND THESE BAGS FOR THE NEXT FOUR HOURS...
BACK-PACK TO SCH
LINCOLN! COME ON! WE'RE GOING SHOE SHOPPING NEXT!
THEY'VE GOT CLOGS IN YOUR SIZE!
I'M NOT WEARING CLOGS!
I GOTTA GET OUT OF HERE!

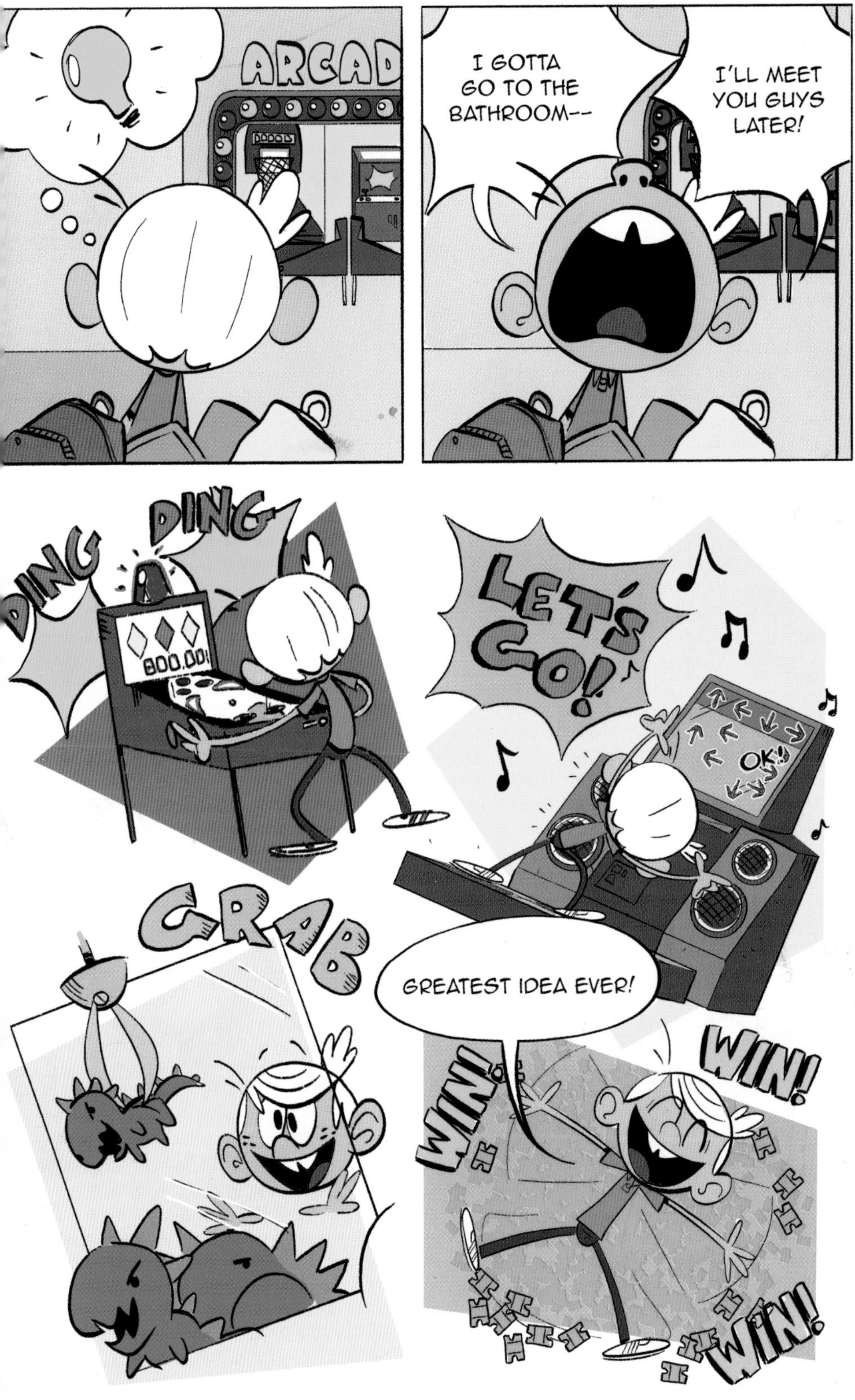
ARCAD
I GOTTA GO TO THE BATHROOM--
I'LL MEET YOU GUYS LATER!
DING DING
800,00!
LET'S GO!
OK!
GRAB
GREATEST IDEA EVER!
WIN!
WIN!
WIN!

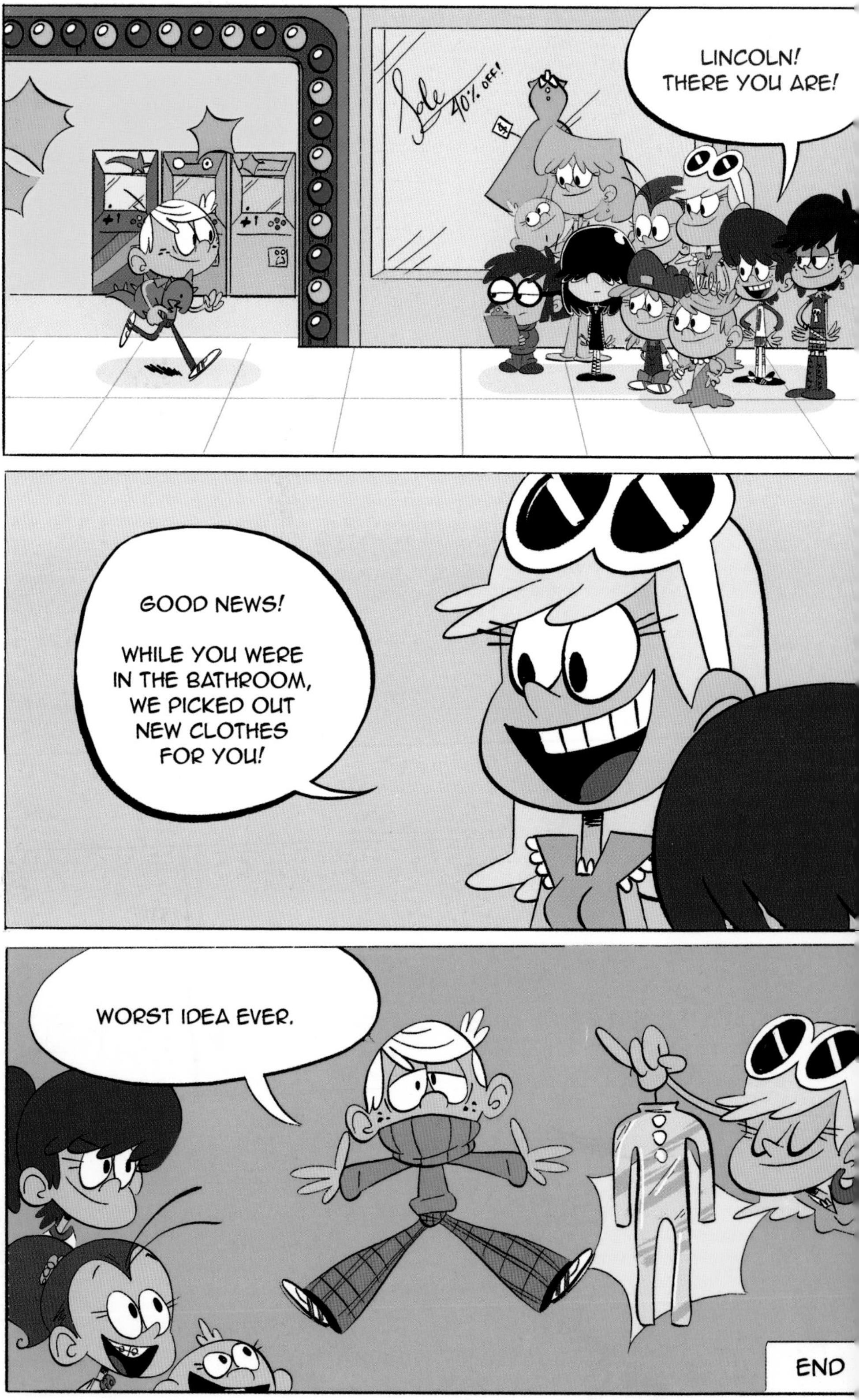
Sale 40% OFF!
LINCOLN! THERE YOU ARE!
GOOD NEWS!
WHILE YOU WERE IN THE BATHROOM, WE PICKED OUT NEW CLOTHES FOR YOU!
WORST IDEA EVER.
END

"POPSICLE PROBLEMS"

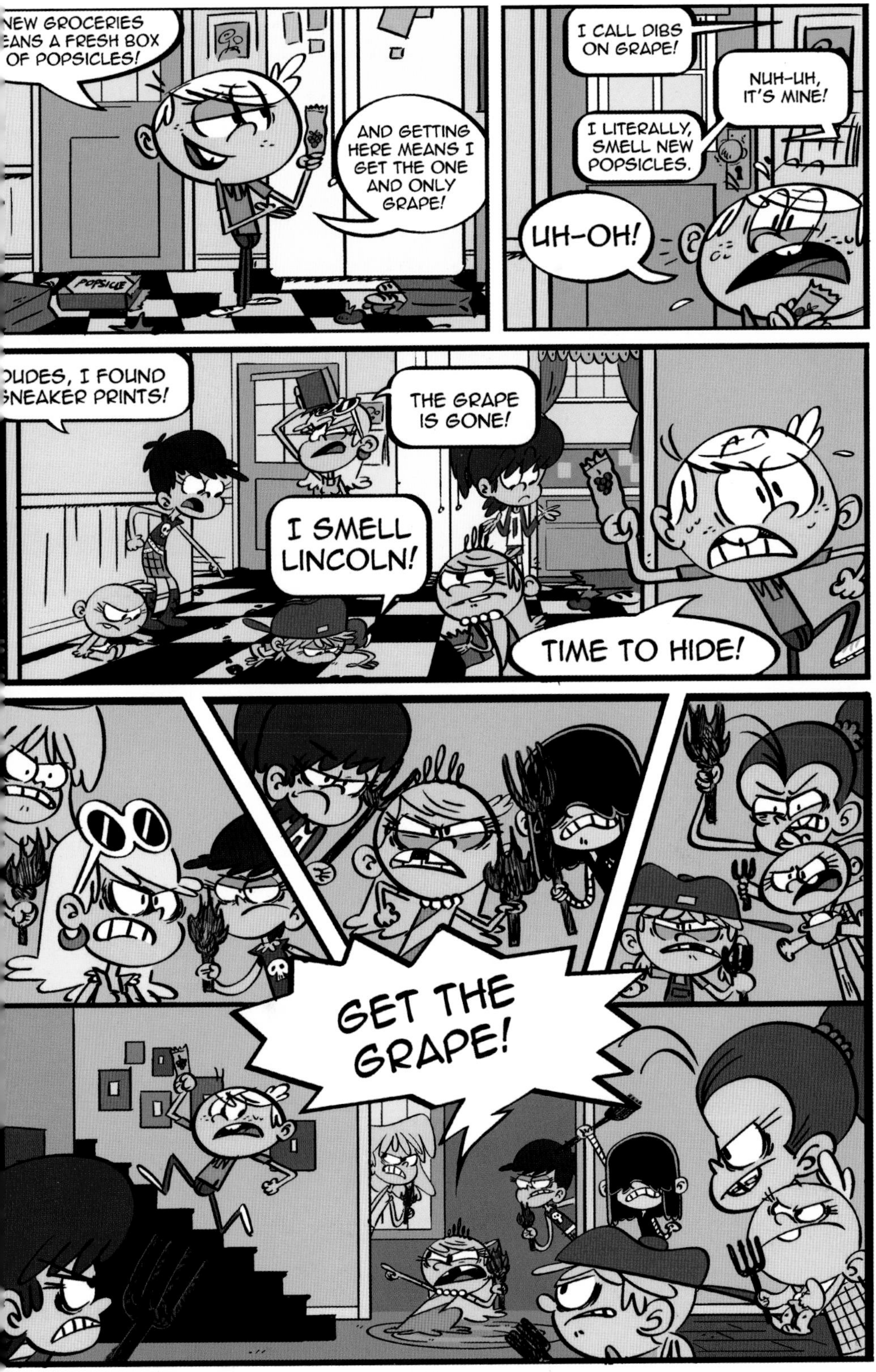

NEW GROCERIES
MEANS A FRESH BOX
OF POPSICLES!
AND GETTING HERE MEANS I GET THE ONE AND ONLY GRAPE!
POPSICLE
I CALL DIBS ON GRAPE!
NUH-UH, IT'S MINE!
I LITERALLY, SMELL NEW POPSICLES.
UH-OH!
DUDES, I FOUND SNEAKER PRINTS!
THE GRAPE IS GONE!
I SMELL LINCOLN!
TIME TO HIDE!
GET THE GRAPE!

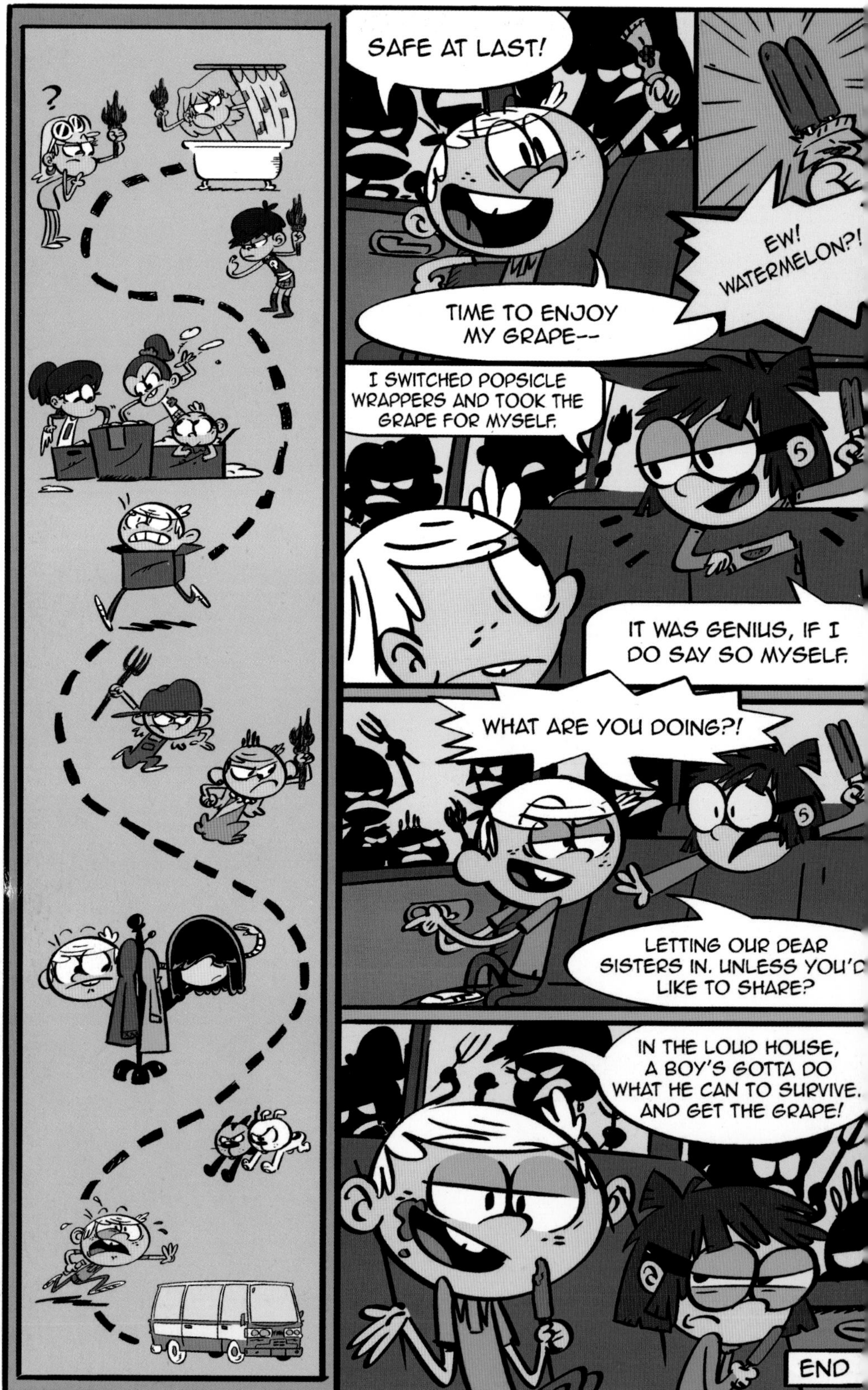
?
SAFE AT LAST!
TIME TO ENJOY MY GRAPE--
EW! WATERMELON?!
I SWITCHED POPSICLE WRAPPERS AND TOOK THE GRAPE FOR MYSELF.
IT WAS GENIUS, IF I DO SAY SO MYSELF.
WHAT ARE YOU DOING?!
LETTING OUR DEAR SISTERS IN. UNLESS YOU'D LIKE TO SHARE?
IN THE LOUD HOUSE, A BOY'S GOTTA DO WHAT HE CAN TO SURVIVE. AND GET THE GRAPE!
END

"HOPPILY EVER AFTER"

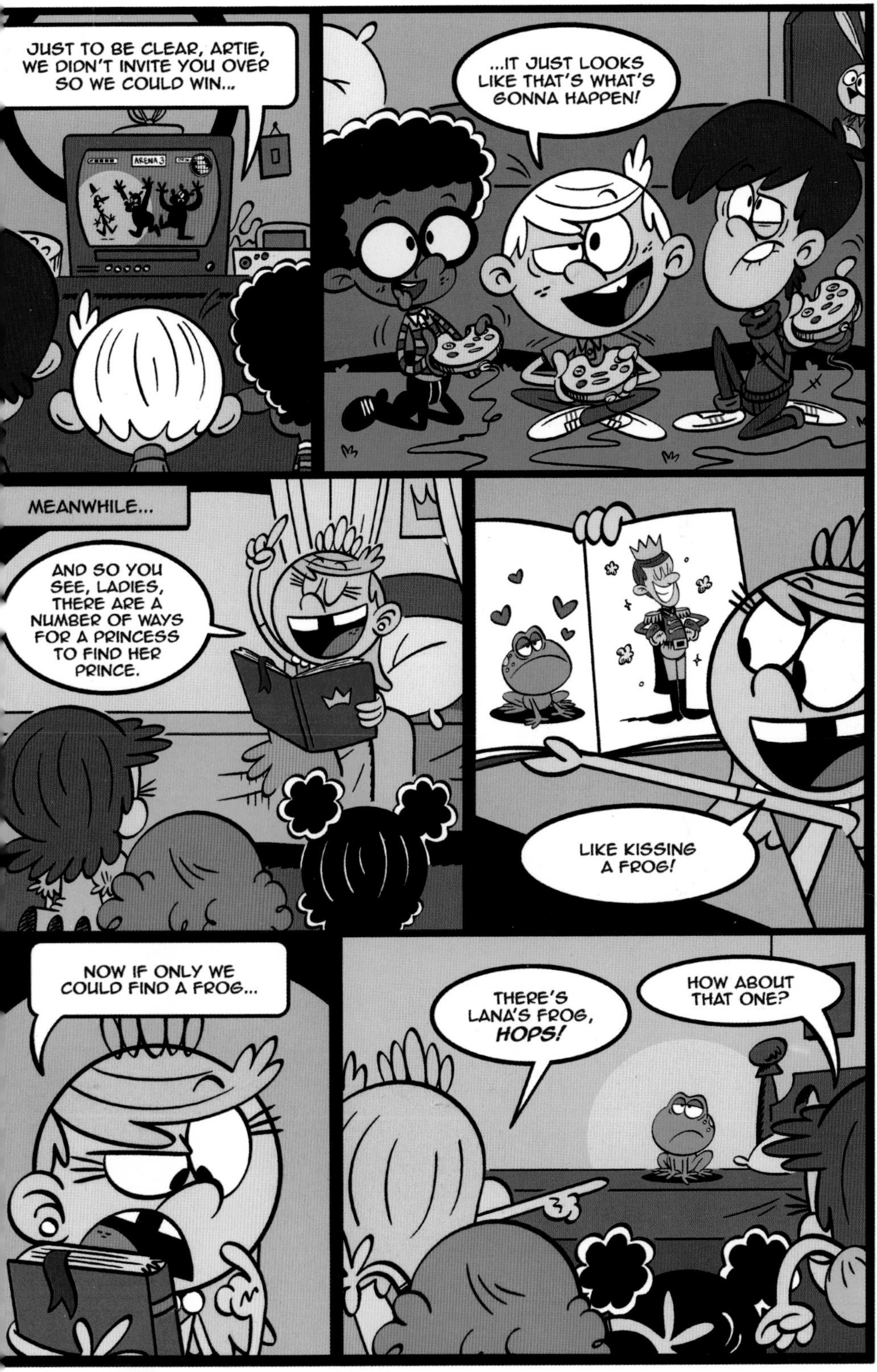
JUST TO BE CLEAR, ARTIE, WE DIDN'T INVITE YOU OVER SO WE COULD WIN...
ARENA 3
...IT JUST LOOKS LIKE THAT'S WHAT'S GONNA HAPPEN!
MEANWHILE...
AND SO YOU SEE, LADIES, THERE ARE A NUMBER OF WAYS FOR A PRINCESS TO FIND HER PRINCE.
LIKE KISSING A FROG!
NOW IF ONLY WE COULD FIND A FROG...
THERE'S LANA'S FROG, *HOPS!*
HOW ABOUT THAT ONE?

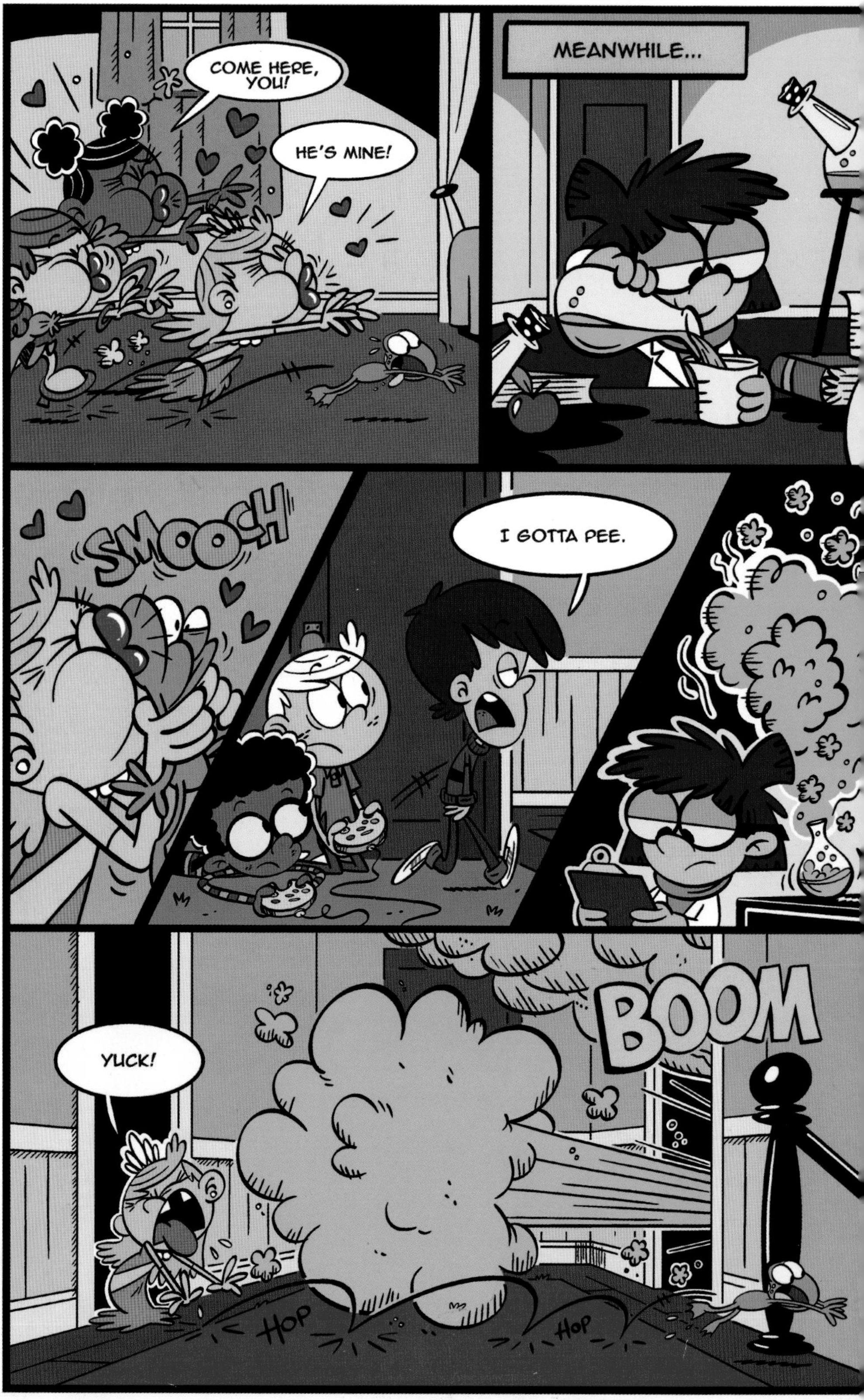
COME HERE, YOU!
HE'S MINE!
MEANWHILE...
SMOOCH
I GOTTA PEE.
YUCK!
BOOM
HOP
HOP

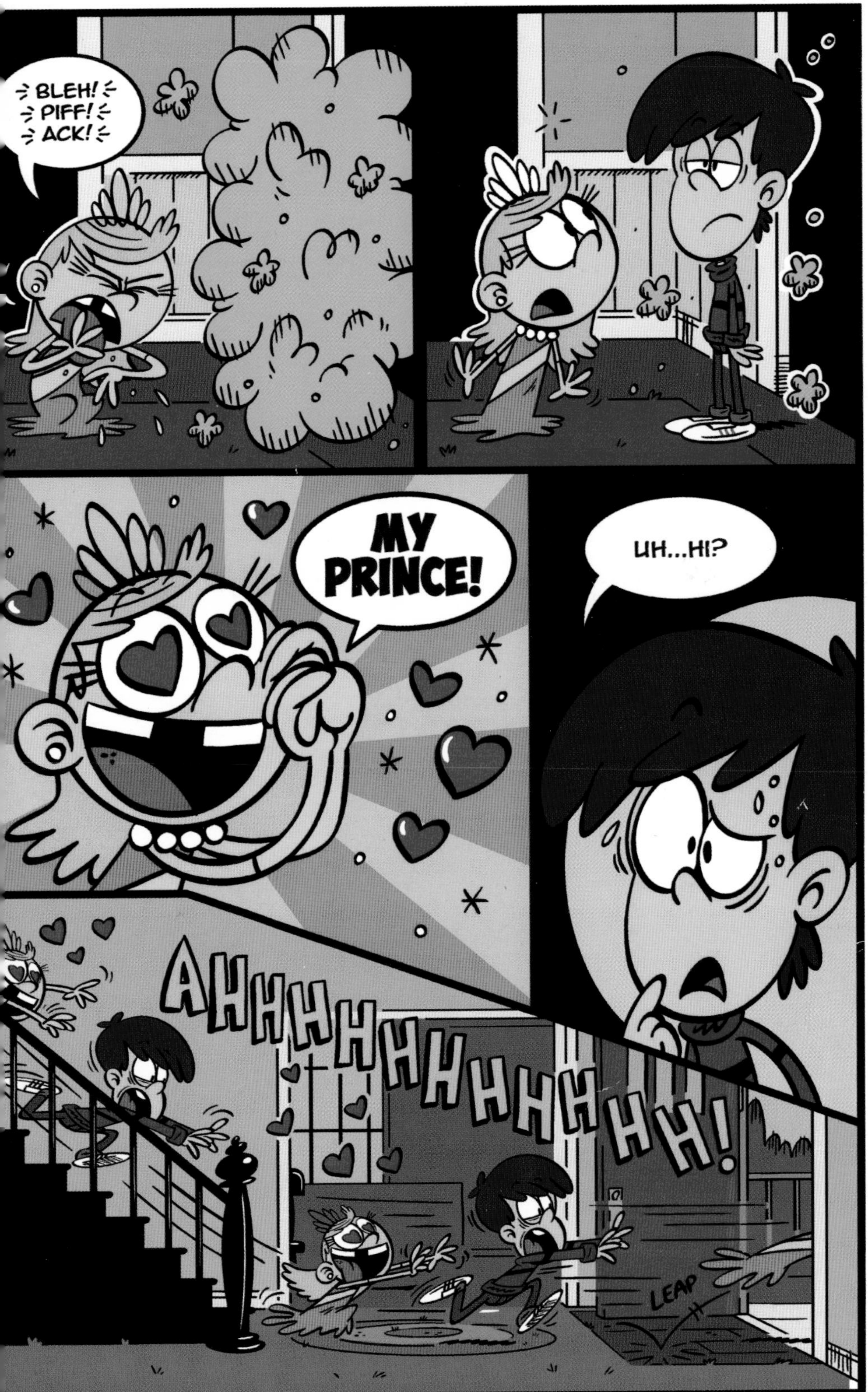
BLEH! PIFF! ACK!
MY PRINCE!
UH...HI?
AHHHHHHHHHHHHH!
LEAP

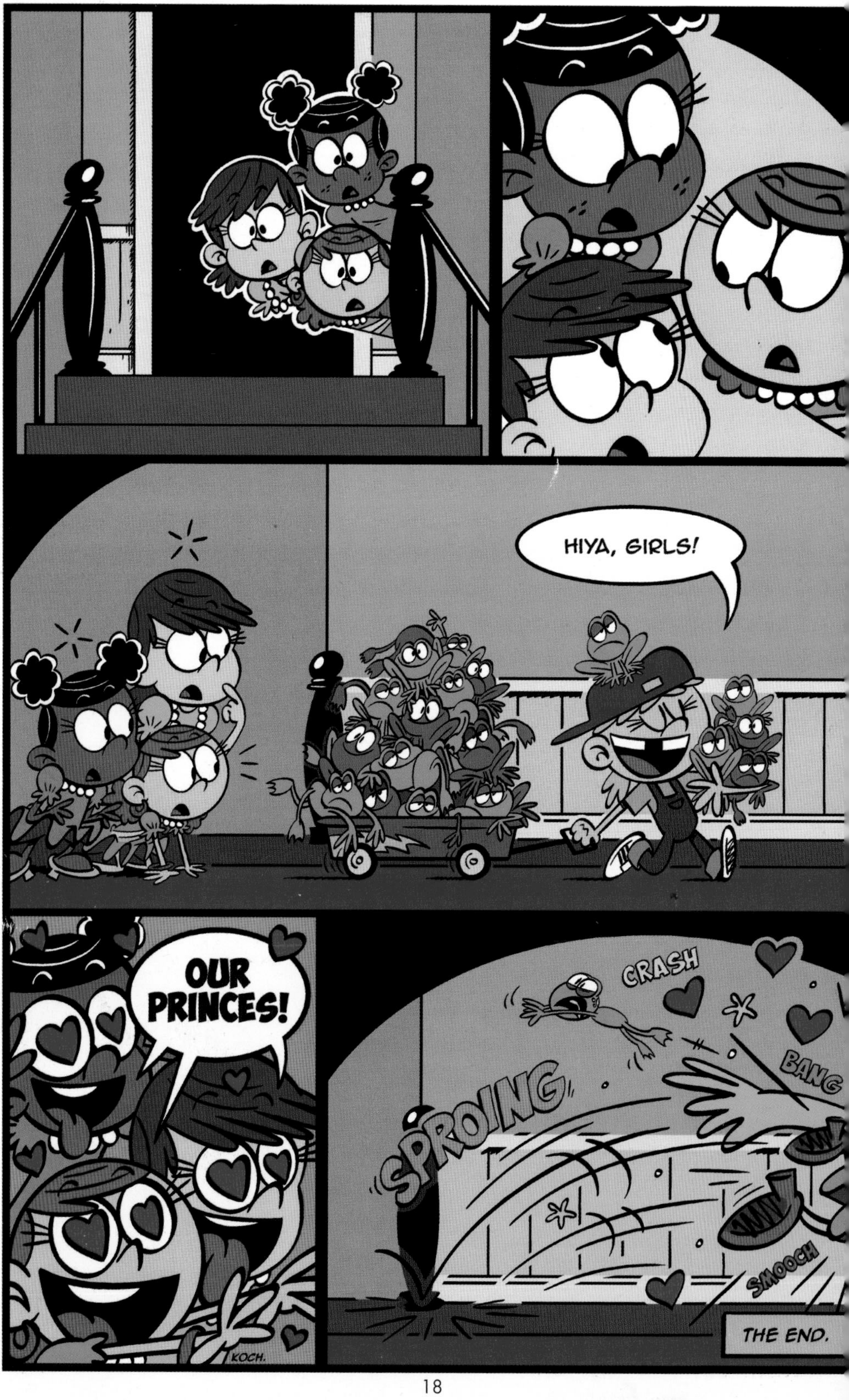
HIYA, GIRLS!
OUR PRINCES!
KOCH.
CRASH
BANG
SPROING
SMOOCH
THE END.

"DATE NIGHT"

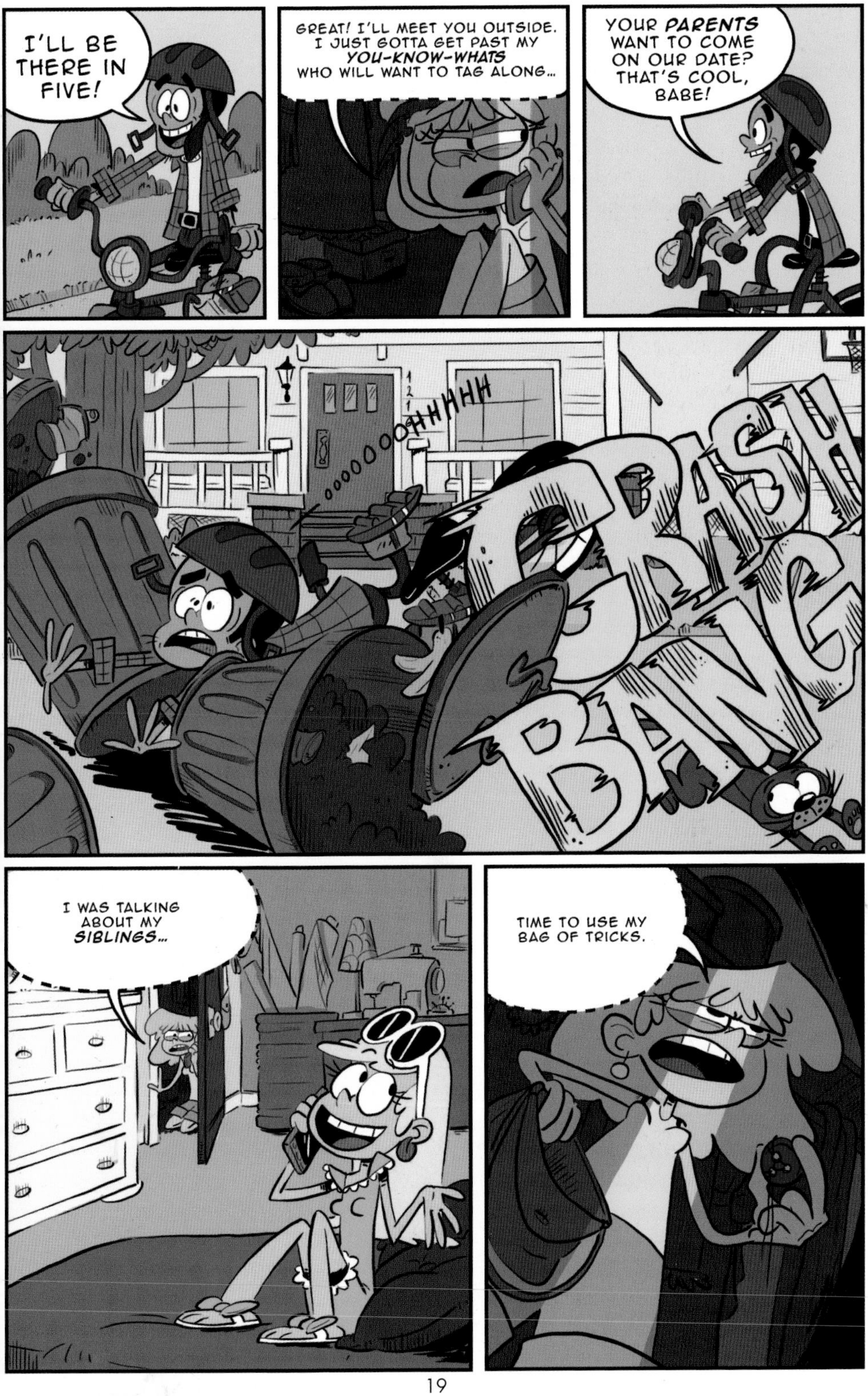

I'LL BE THERE IN FIVE!
GREAT! I'LL MEET YOU OUTSIDE. I JUST GOTTA GET PAST MY *YOU-KNOW-WHATS* WHO WILL WANT TO TAG ALONG...
YOUR *PARENTS* WANT TO COME ON OUR DATE? THAT'S COOL, BABE!
OOOOOOOHHHHH
CRASH
BANG
I WAS TALKING ABOUT MY *SIBLINGS*...
TIME TO USE MY BAG OF TRICKS.

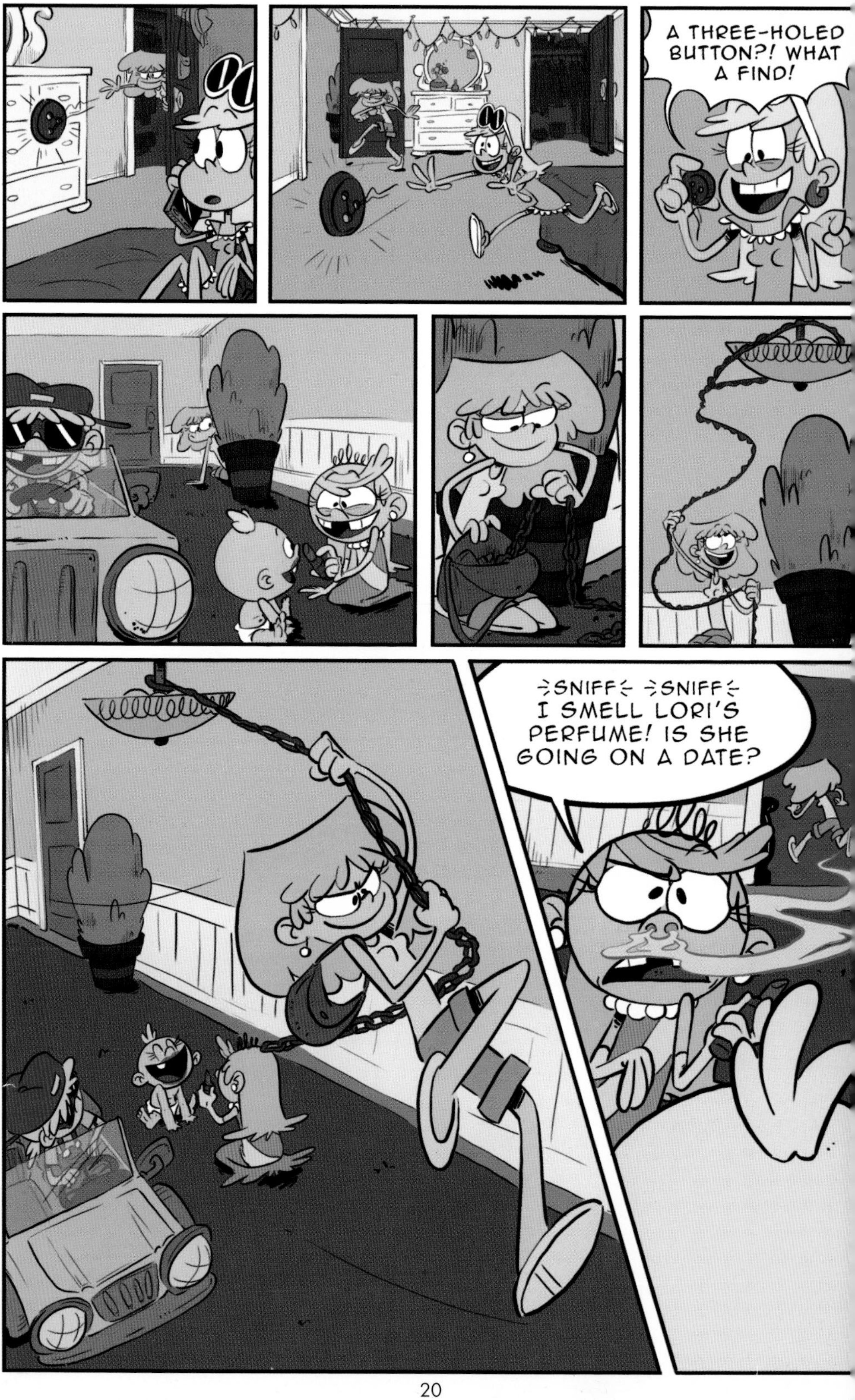
A THREE-HOLED BUTTON?! WHAT A FIND!
SNIFF SNIFF I SMELL LORI'S PERFUME! IS SHE GOING ON A DATE?

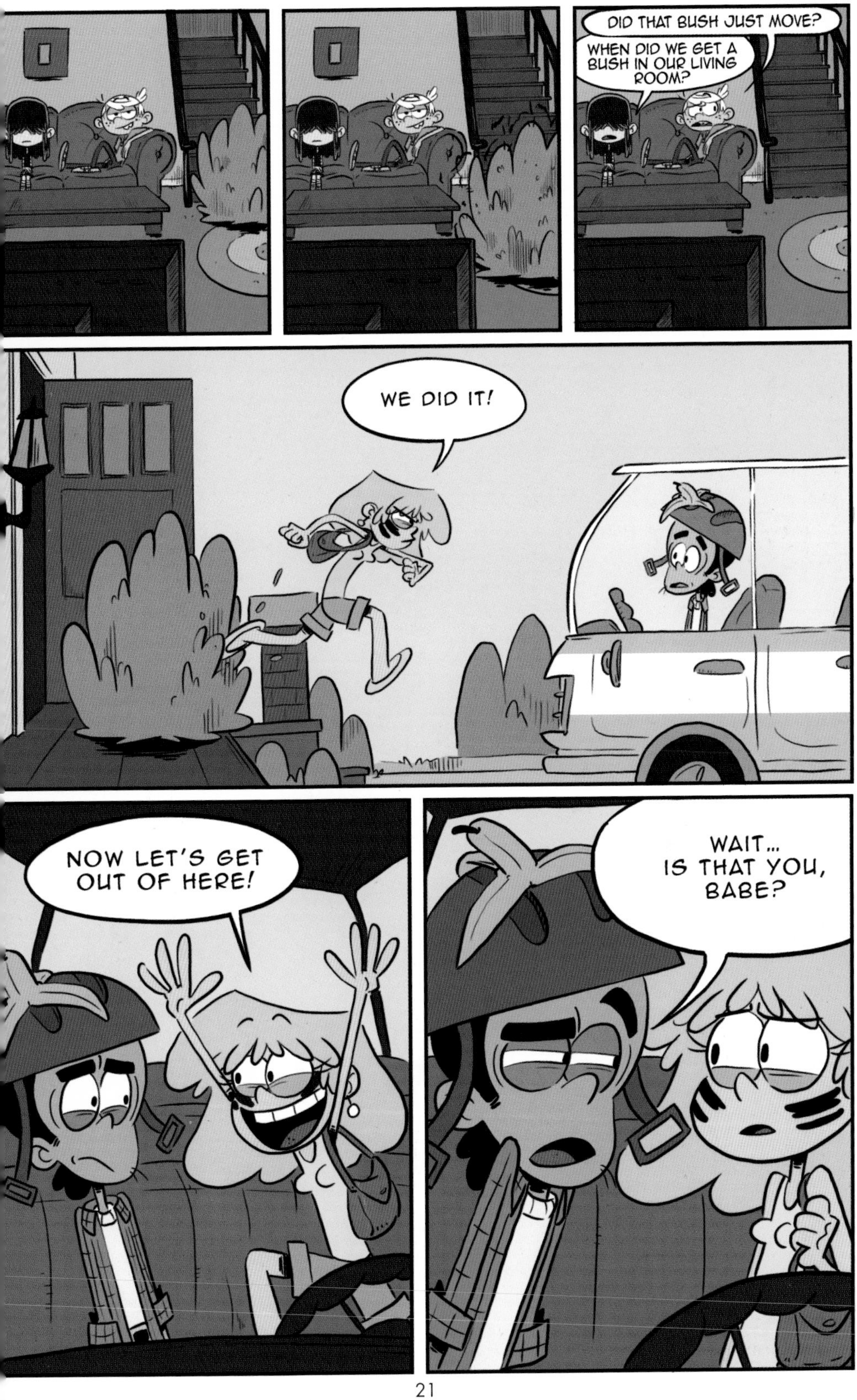
DID THAT BUSH JUST MOVE?
WHEN DID WE GET A BUSH IN OUR LIVING ROOM?
WE DID IT!
NOW LET'S GET OUT OF HERE!
WAIT... IS THAT YOU, BABE?

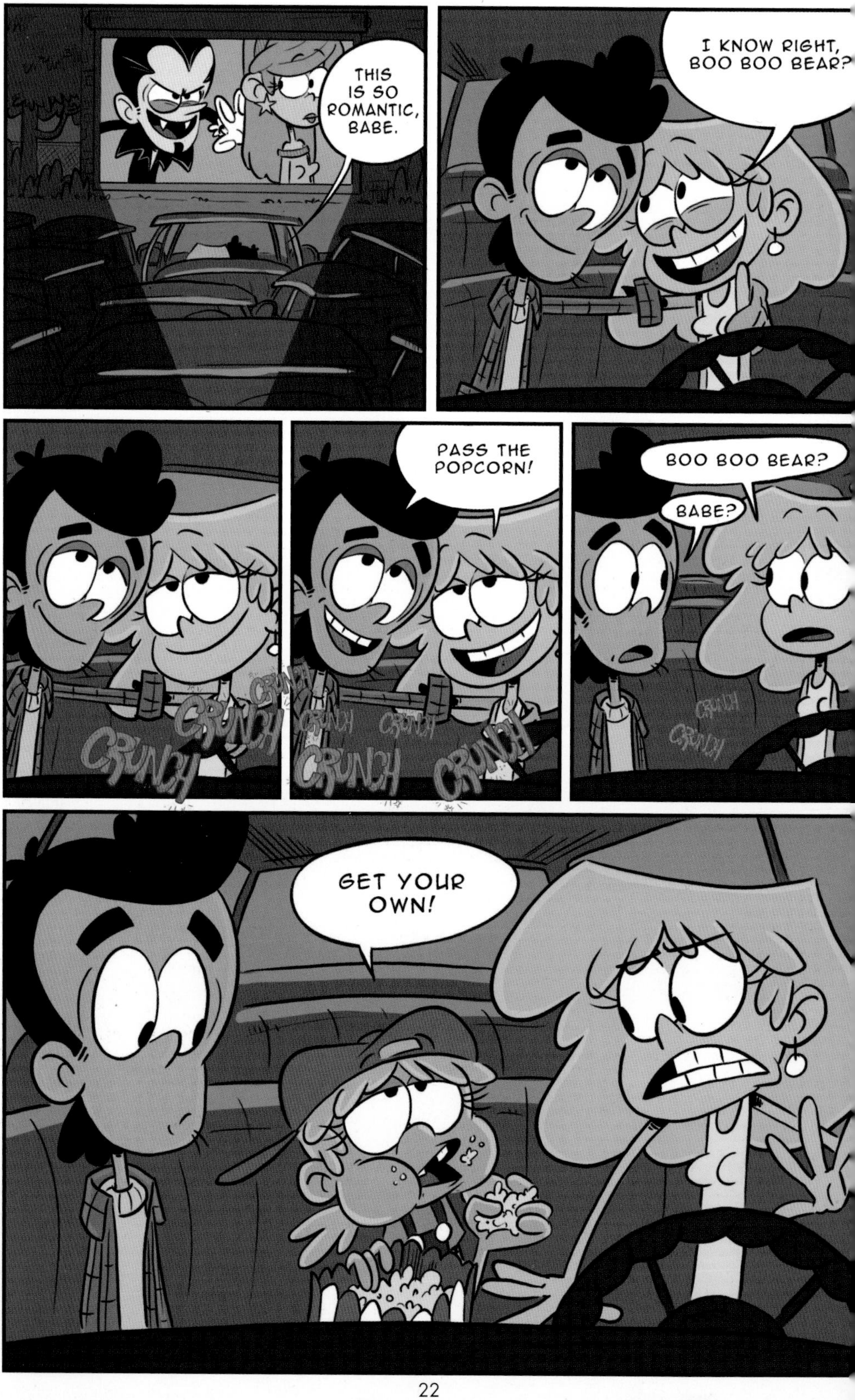

THIS IS SO ROMANTIC, BABE.
I KNOW RIGHT, BOO BOO BEAR?
CRUNCH
CRUNCH
CRUNCH
PASS THE POPCORN!
CRUNCH
CRUNCH
CRUNCH
CRUNCH
BOO BOO BEAR?
BABE?
CRUNCH
CRUNCH
GET YOUR OWN!

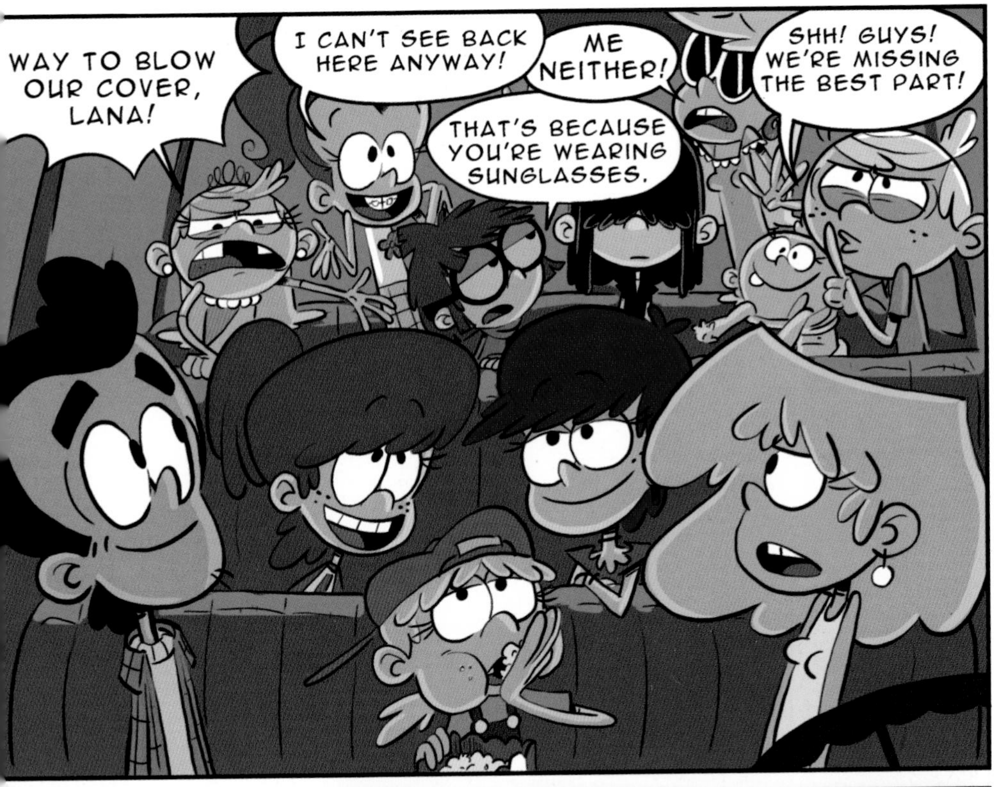
WAY TO BLOW OUR COVER, LANA!
I CAN'T SEE BACK HERE ANYWAY!
ME NEITHER!
SHH! GUYS! WE'RE MISSING THE BEST PART!
THAT'S BECAUSE YOU'RE WEARING SUNGLASSES.

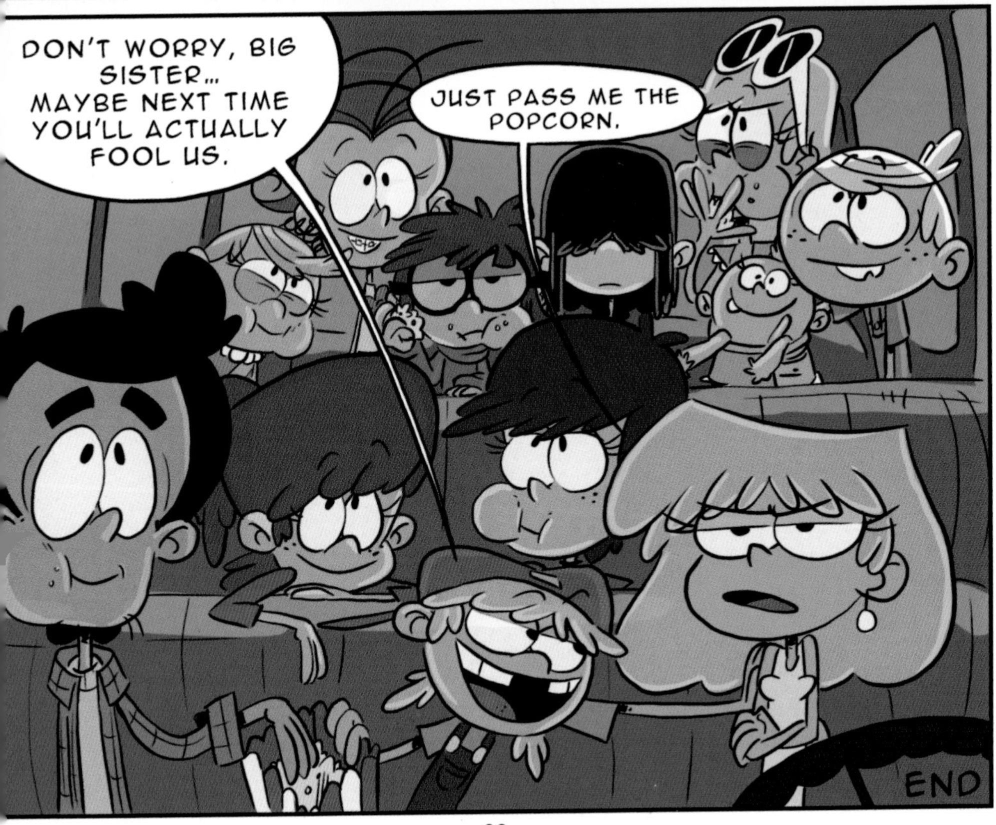
DON'T WORRY, BIG SISTER... MAYBE NEXT TIME YOU'LL ACTUALLY FOOL US.
JUST PASS ME THE POPCORN.
END

"THE SNEEZE!"

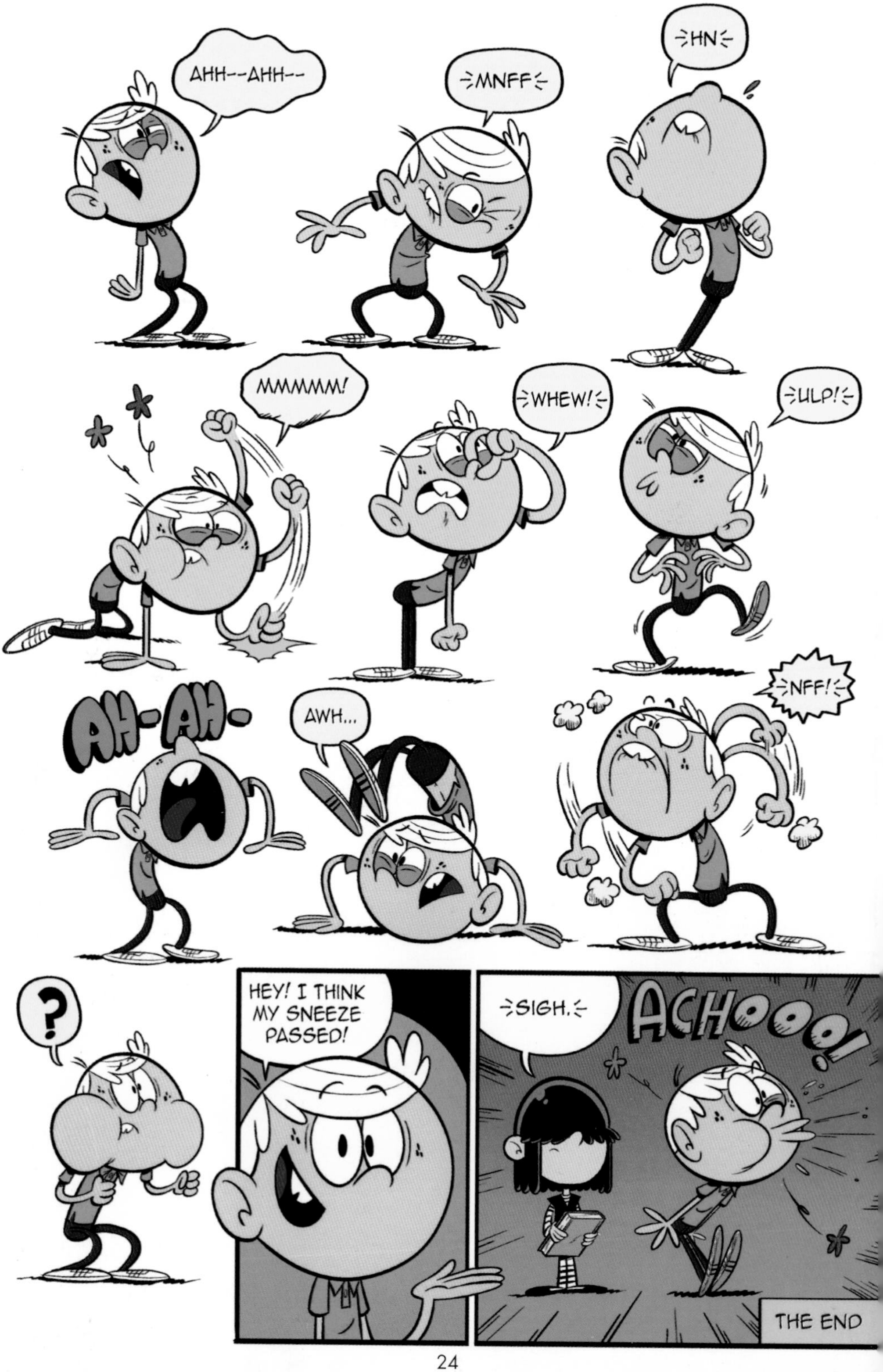
AHH--AHH--
MNFF
HN
MMMMM!
WHEW!
ULP!
AH-AH-
AWH...
NFF!
?
HEY! I THINK MY SNEEZE PASSED!
SIGH.
ACHOOOO!
THE END

"CLYDE'S CAT-ASTROPHE"

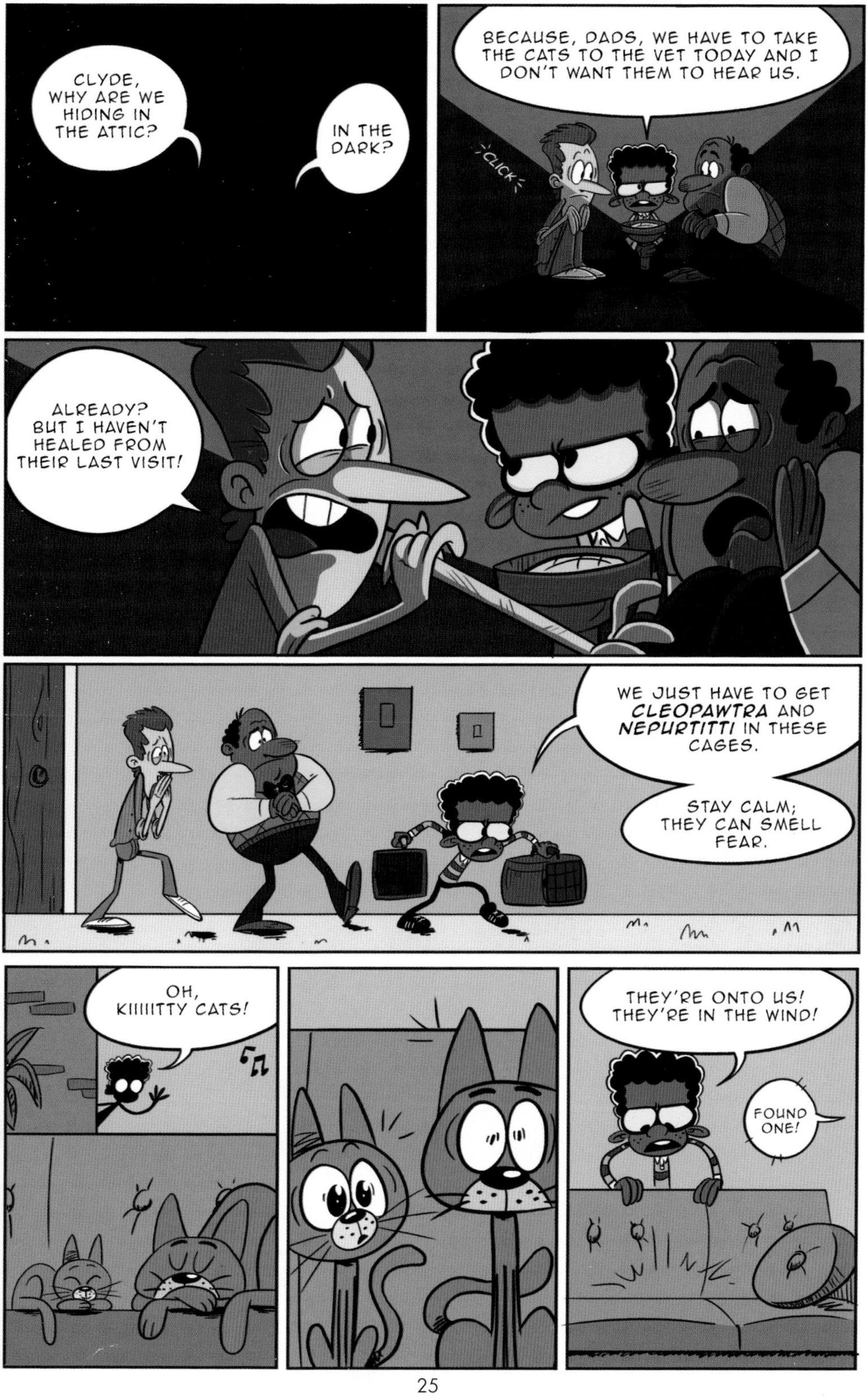
CLYDE, WHY ARE WE HIDING IN THE ATTIC?
IN THE DARK?
BECAUSE, DADS, WE HAVE TO TAKE THE CATS TO THE VET TODAY AND I DON'T WANT THEM TO HEAR US.
CLICK
ALREADY? BUT I HAVEN'T HEALED FROM THEIR LAST VISIT!
WE JUST HAVE TO GET CLEOPAWTRA AND NEPURTITTI IN THESE CAGES.
STAY CALM; THEY CAN SMELL FEAR.
OH, KIIIIITTY CATS!
THEY'RE ONTO US! THEY'RE IN THE WIND!
FOUND ONE!

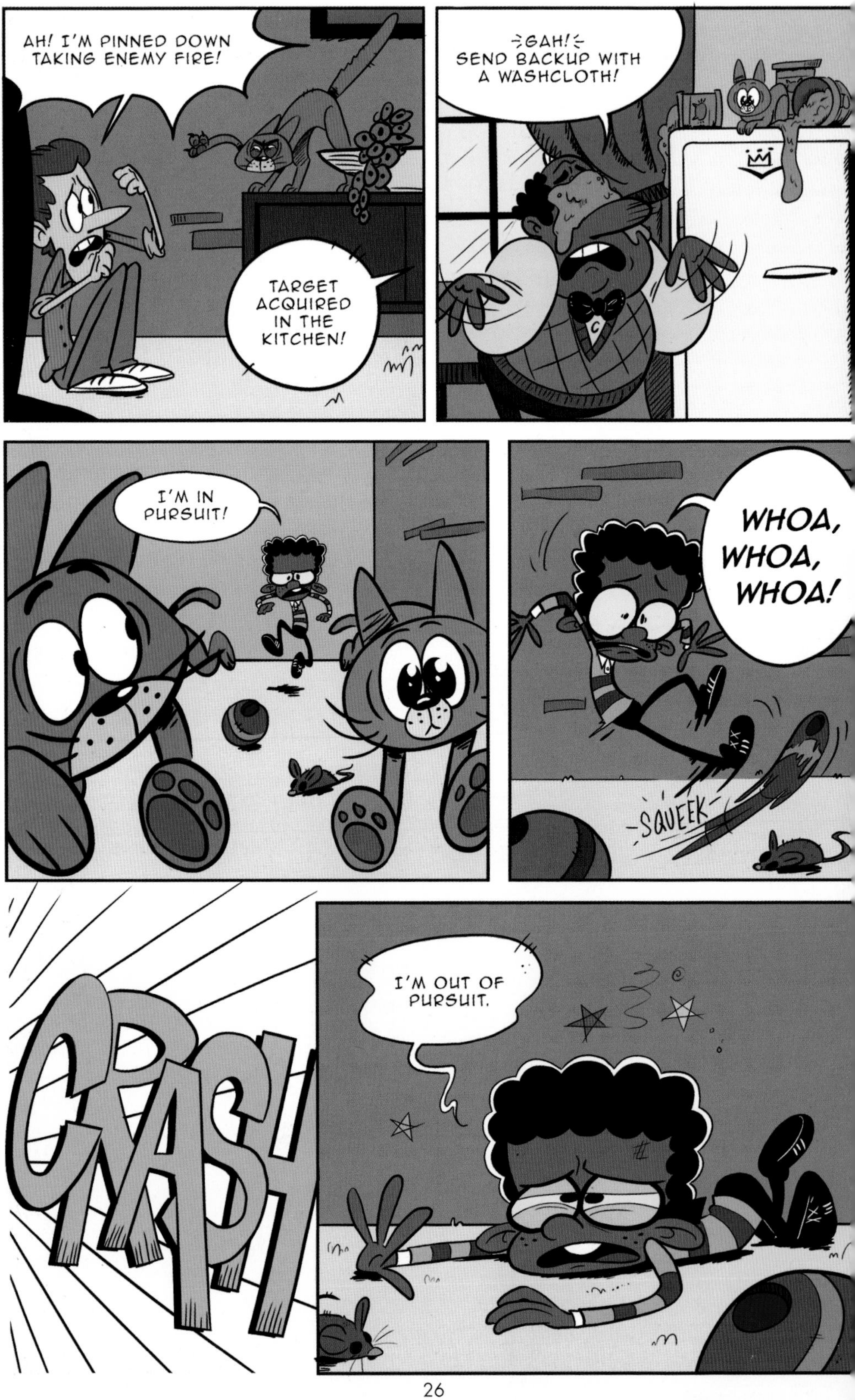
AH! I'M PINNED DOWN TAKING ENEMY FIRE!
TARGET ACQUIRED IN THE KITCHEN!
GAH!
SEND BACKUP WITH A WASHCLOTH!
I'M IN PURSUIT!
WHOA, WHOA, WHOA!
SQUEEK
CRASH
I'M OUT OF PURSUIT.

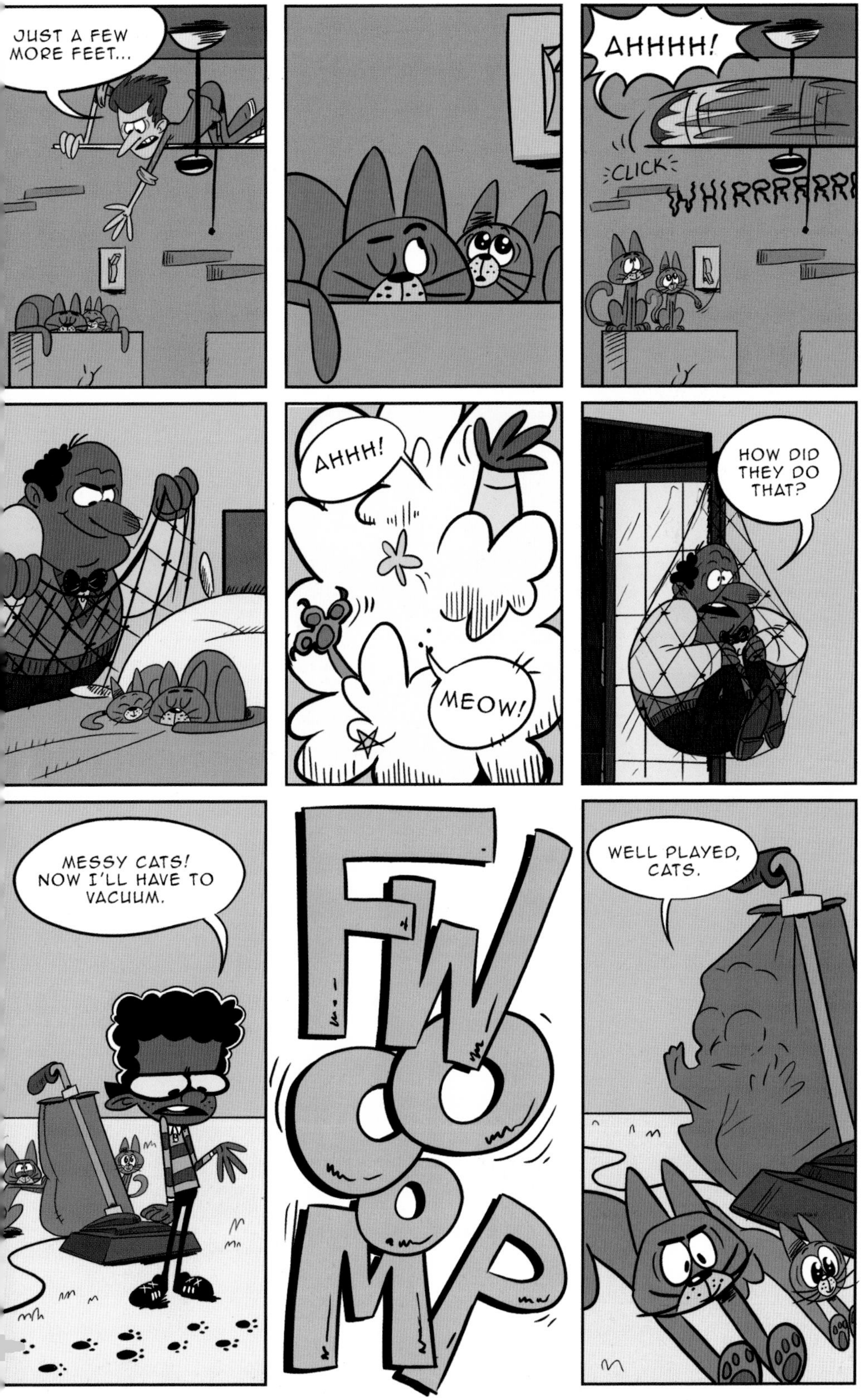

JUST A FEW MORE FEET...
AHHHH!
CLICK
WHIRRRRRR
AHHH!
MEOW!
HOW DID THEY DO THAT?
MESSY CATS! NOW I'LL HAVE TO VACUUM.
FWOOOMP
WELL PLAYED, CATS.

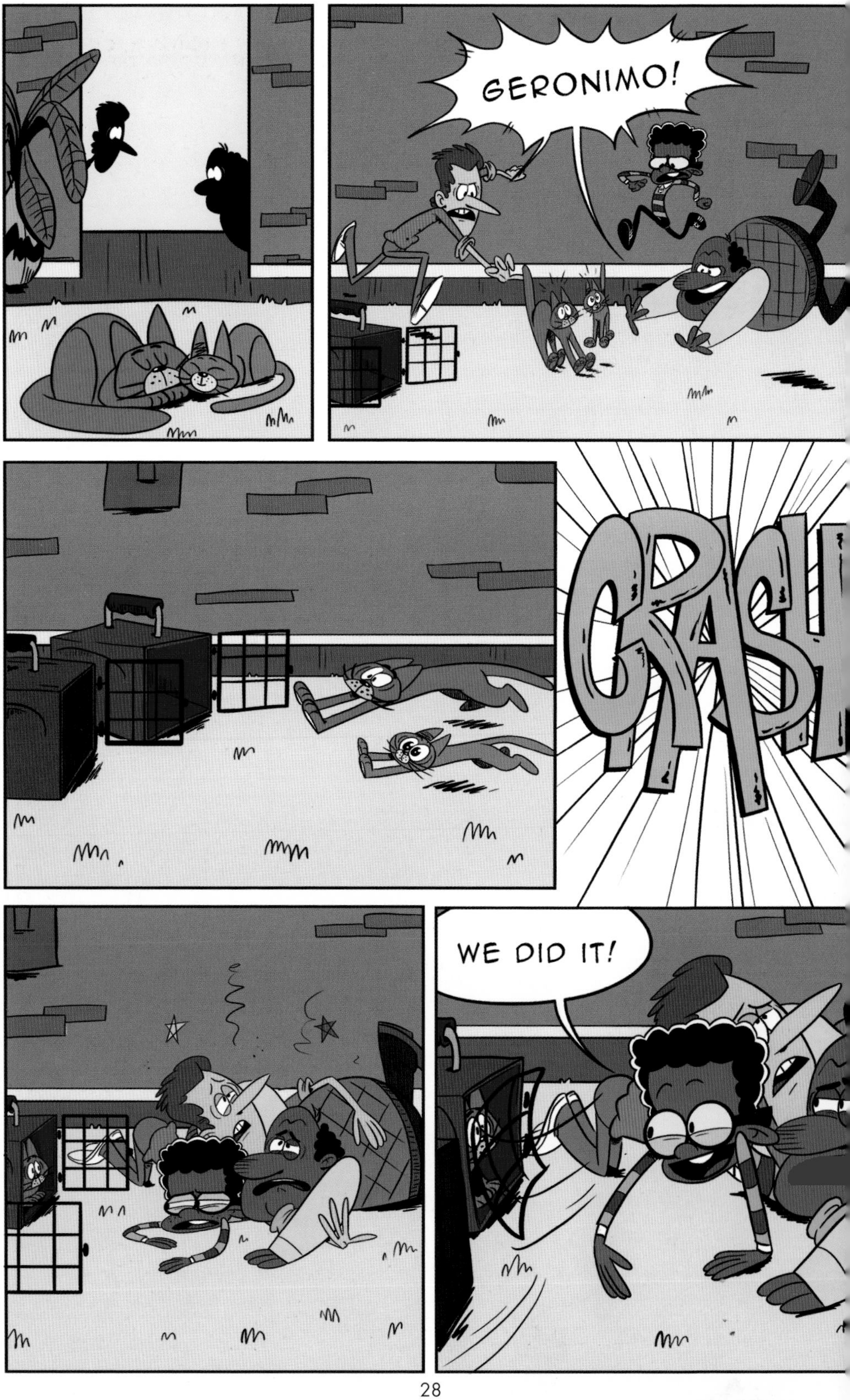
GERONIMO!
CRASH
WE DID IT!

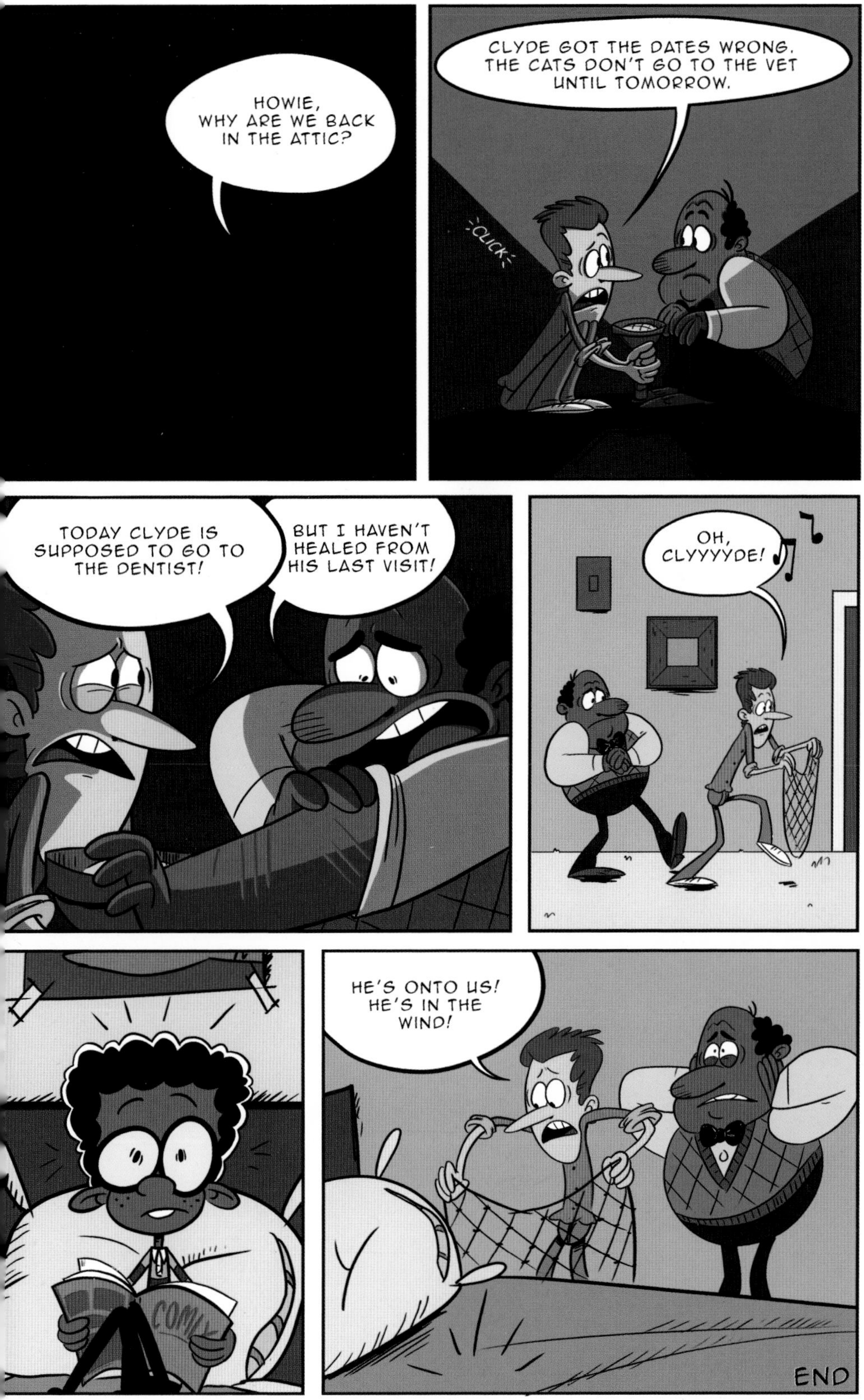
HOWIE, WHY ARE WE BACK IN THE ATTIC?
CLYDE GOT THE DATES WRONG. THE CATS DON'T GO TO THE VET UNTIL TOMORROW.
CLICK
TODAY CLYDE IS SUPPOSED TO GO TO THE DENTIST!
BUT I HAVEN'T HEALED FROM HIS LAST VISIT!
OH, CLYYYYDE!
HE'S ONTO US! HE'S IN THE WIND!
END

"LAND ESCAPE"

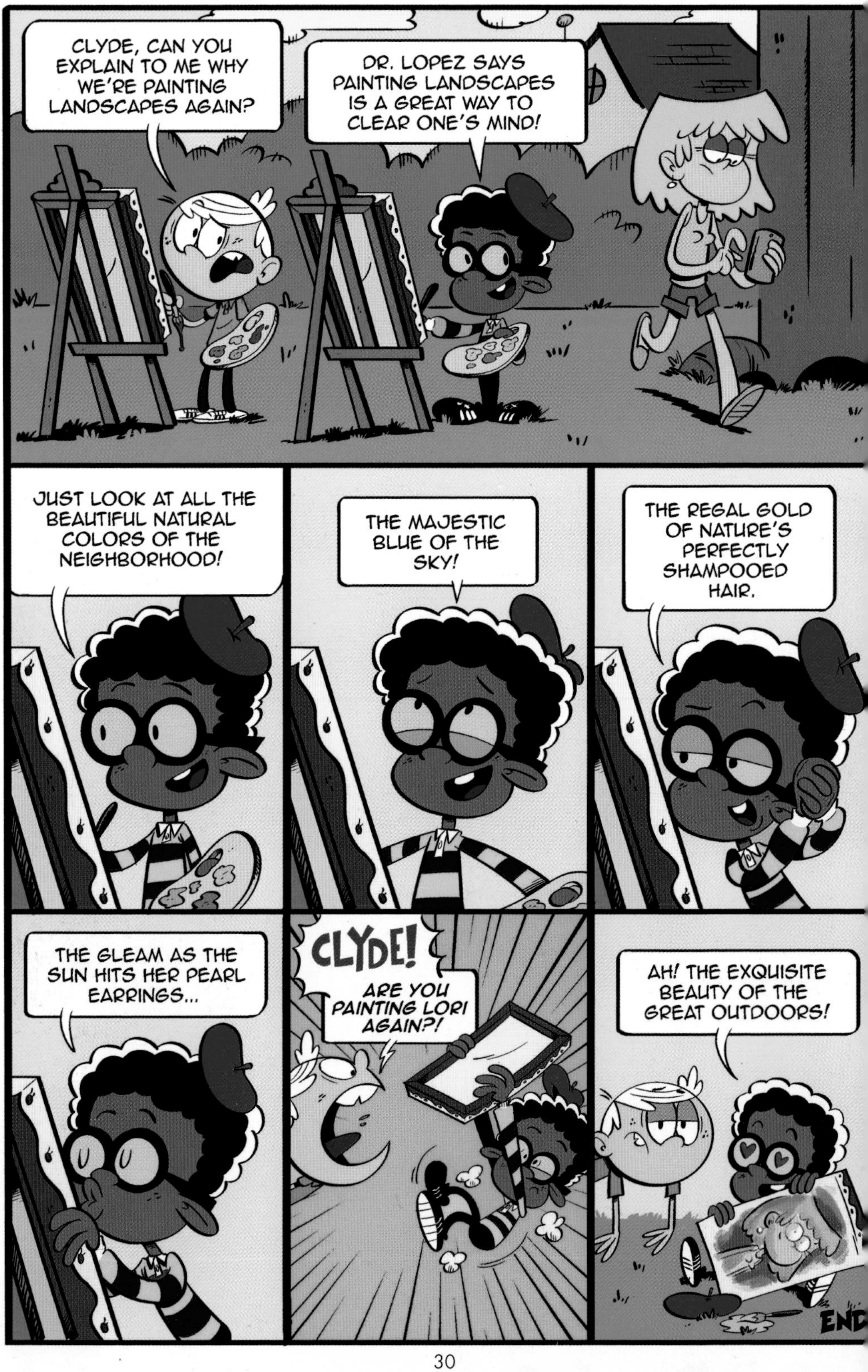
CLYDE, CAN YOU EXPLAIN TO ME WHY WE'RE PAINTING LANDSCAPES AGAIN?
DR. LOPEZ SAYS PAINTING LANDSCAPES IS A GREAT WAY TO CLEAR ONE'S MIND!
JUST LOOK AT ALL THE BEAUTIFUL NATURAL COLORS OF THE NEIGHBORHOOD!
THE MAJESTIC BLUE OF THE SKY!
THE REGAL GOLD OF NATURE'S PERFECTLY SHAMPOOED HAIR.
THE GLEAM AS THE SUN HITS HER PEARL EARRINGS...
CLYDE!
ARE YOU PAINTING LORI AGAIN?!
AH! THE EXQUISITE BEAUTY OF THE GREAT OUTDOORS!
END

"HOUSE TRAINING"

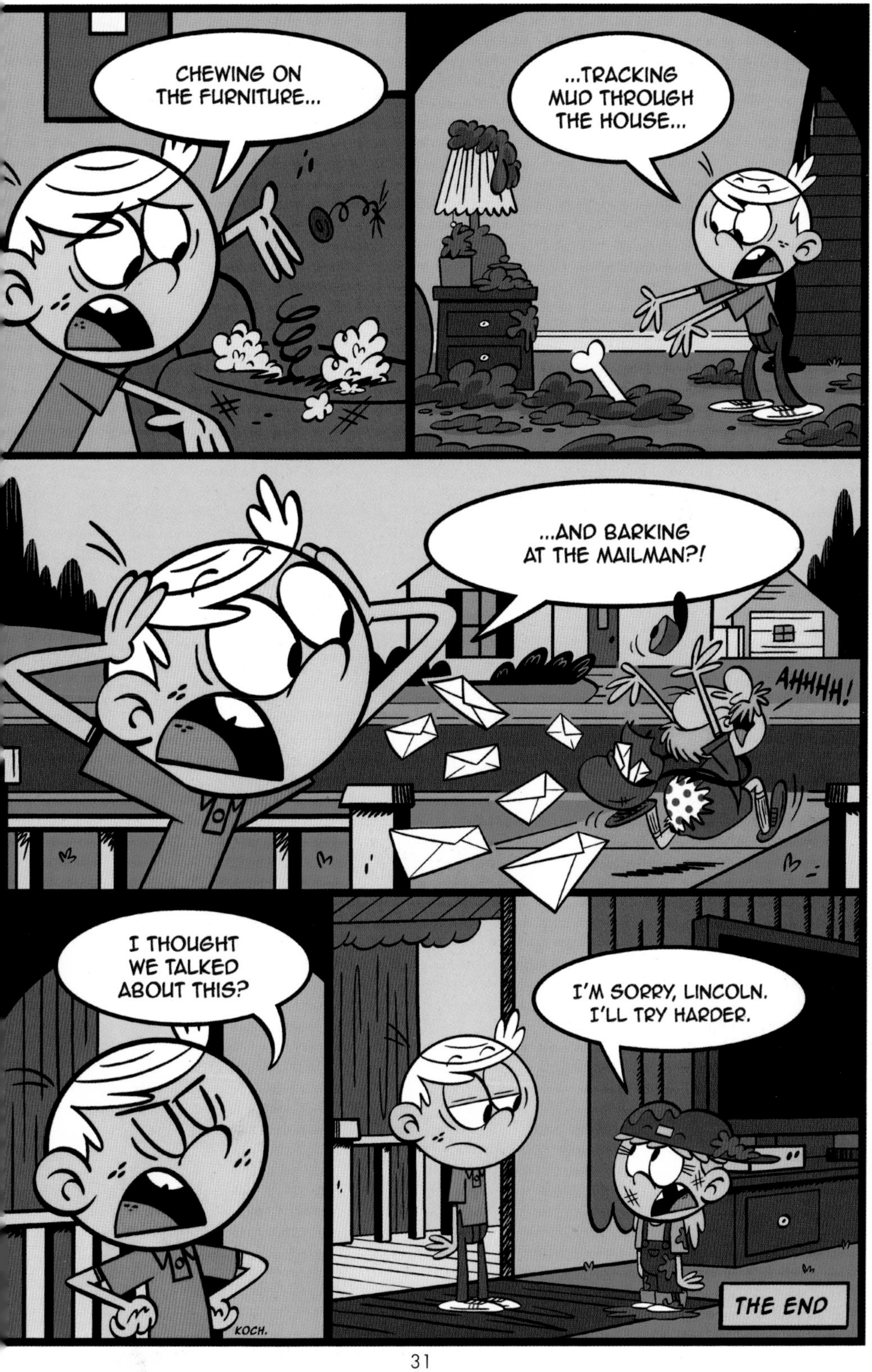
CHEWING ON THE FURNITURE...
...TRACKING MUD THROUGH THE HOUSE...
...AND BARKING AT THE MAILMAN?!
AHHHH!
I THOUGHT WE TALKED ABOUT THIS?
I'M SORRY, LINCOLN. I'LL TRY HARDER.
KOCH.
THE END

"TROPICAL PARADISE"

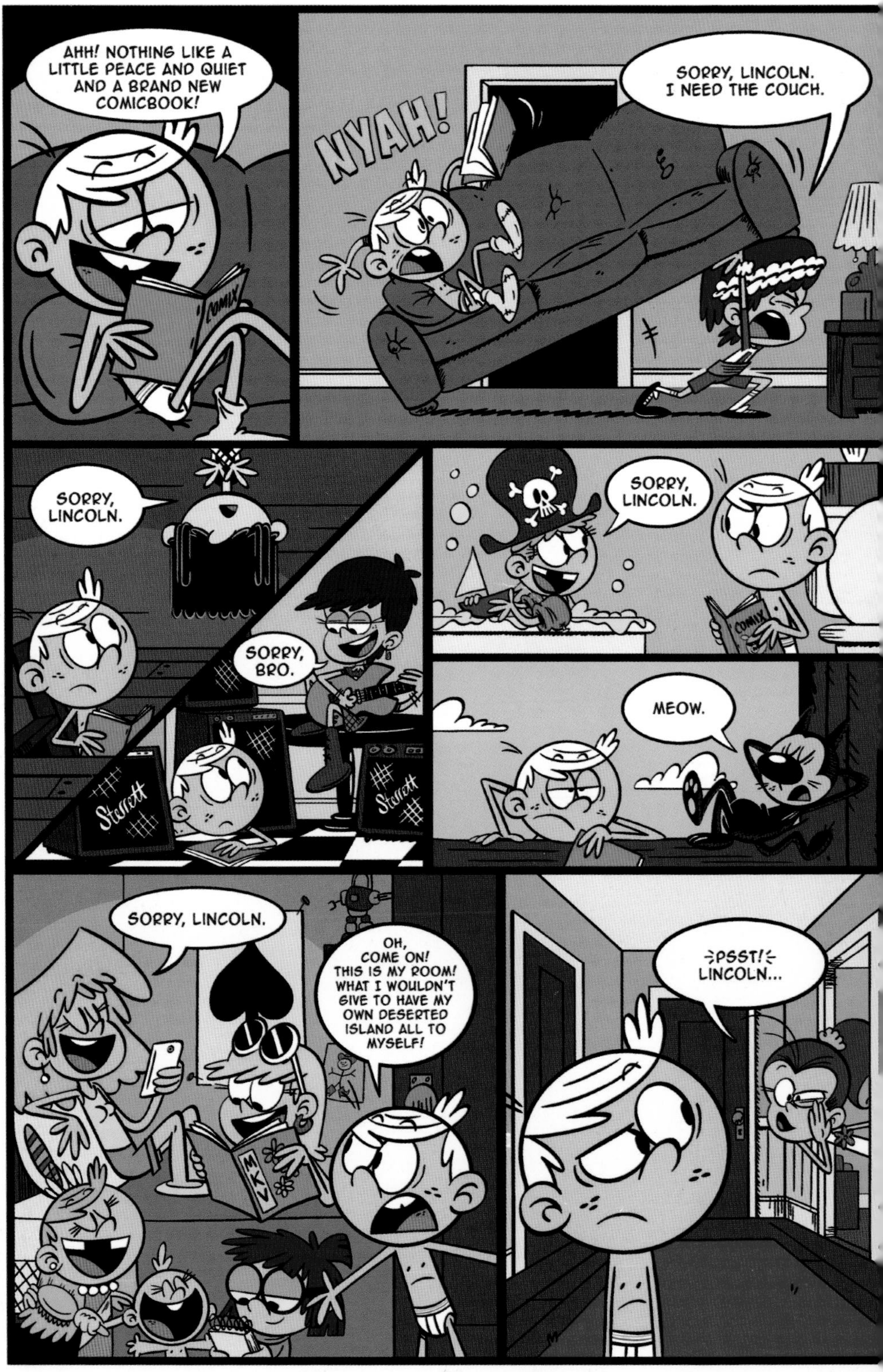
AHH! NOTHING LIKE A LITTLE PEACE AND QUIET AND A BRAND NEW COMICBOOK!
COMIX
NYAH!
SORRY, LINCOLN. I NEED THE COUCH.
SORRY, LINCOLN.
SORRY, BRO.
Sterrett
Sterrett
SORRY, LINCOLN.
COMIX
MEOW.
SORRY, LINCOLN.
OH, COME ON! THIS IS MY ROOM! WHAT I WOULDN'T GIVE TO HAVE MY OWN DESERTED ISLAND ALL TO MYSELF!
MKV
PSST! LINCOLN...

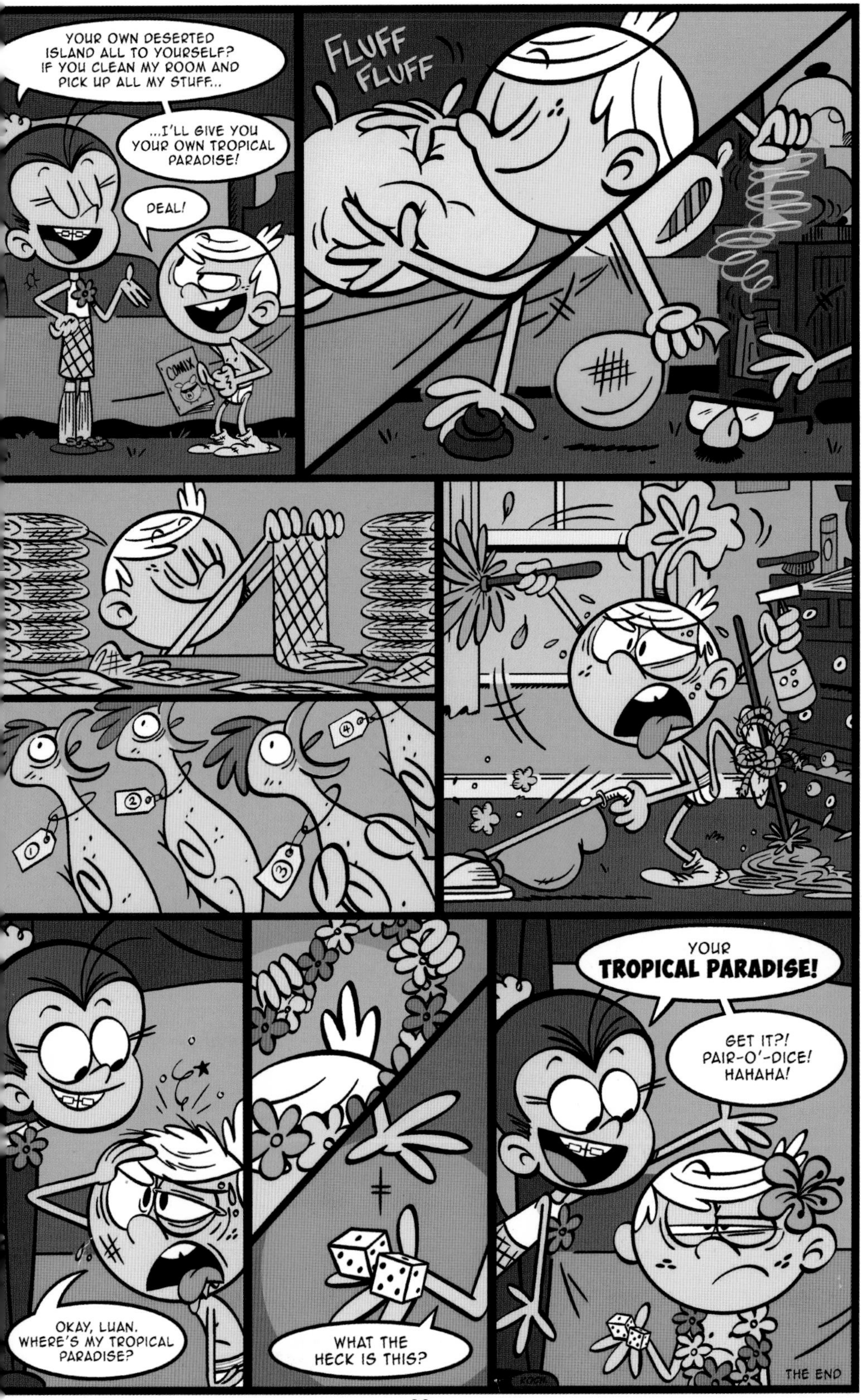
YOUR OWN DESERTED ISLAND ALL TO YOURSELF? IF YOU CLEAN MY ROOM AND PICK UP ALL MY STUFF...
...I'LL GIVE YOU YOUR OWN TROPICAL PARADISE!
DEAL!
COMIX
FLUFF FLUFF
OKAY, LUAN. WHERE'S MY TROPICAL PARADISE?
WHAT THE HECK IS THIS?
YOUR TROPICAL PARADISE!
GET IT?! PAIR-O'-DICE! HAHAHA!
THE END

"TIRED OUT"

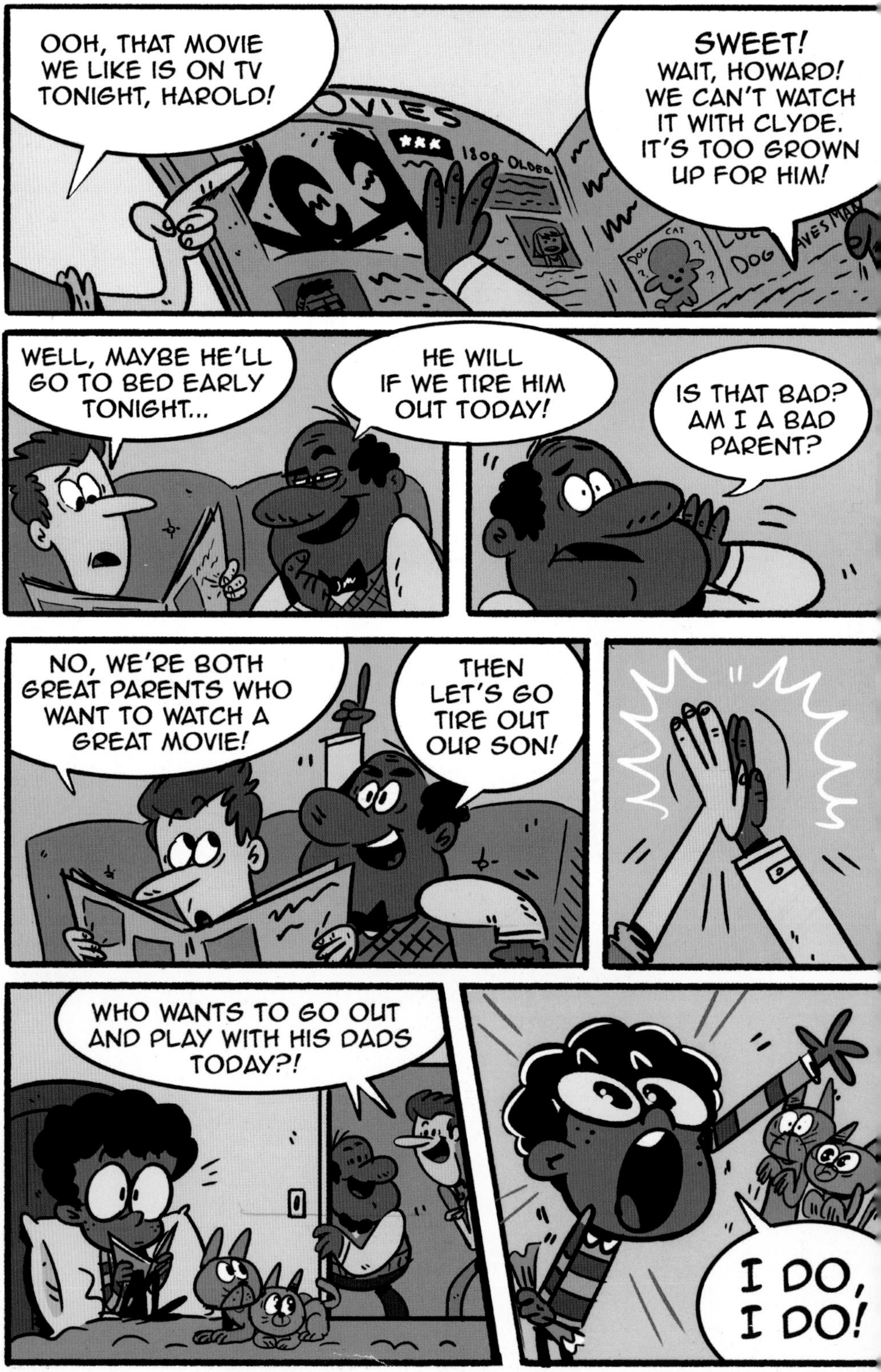
OOH, THAT MOVIE WE LIKE IS ON TV TONIGHT, HAROLD!
SWEET! WAIT, HOWARD! WE CAN'T WATCH IT WITH CLYDE. IT'S TOO GROWN UP FOR HIM!
WELL, MAYBE HE'LL GO TO BED EARLY TONIGHT...
HE WILL IF WE TIRE HIM OUT TODAY!
IS THAT BAD? AM I A BAD PARENT?
NO, WE'RE BOTH GREAT PARENTS WHO WANT TO WATCH A GREAT MOVIE!
THEN LET'S GO TIRE OUT OUR SON!
WHO WANTS TO GO OUT AND PLAY WITH HIS DADS TODAY?!
I DO, I DO!

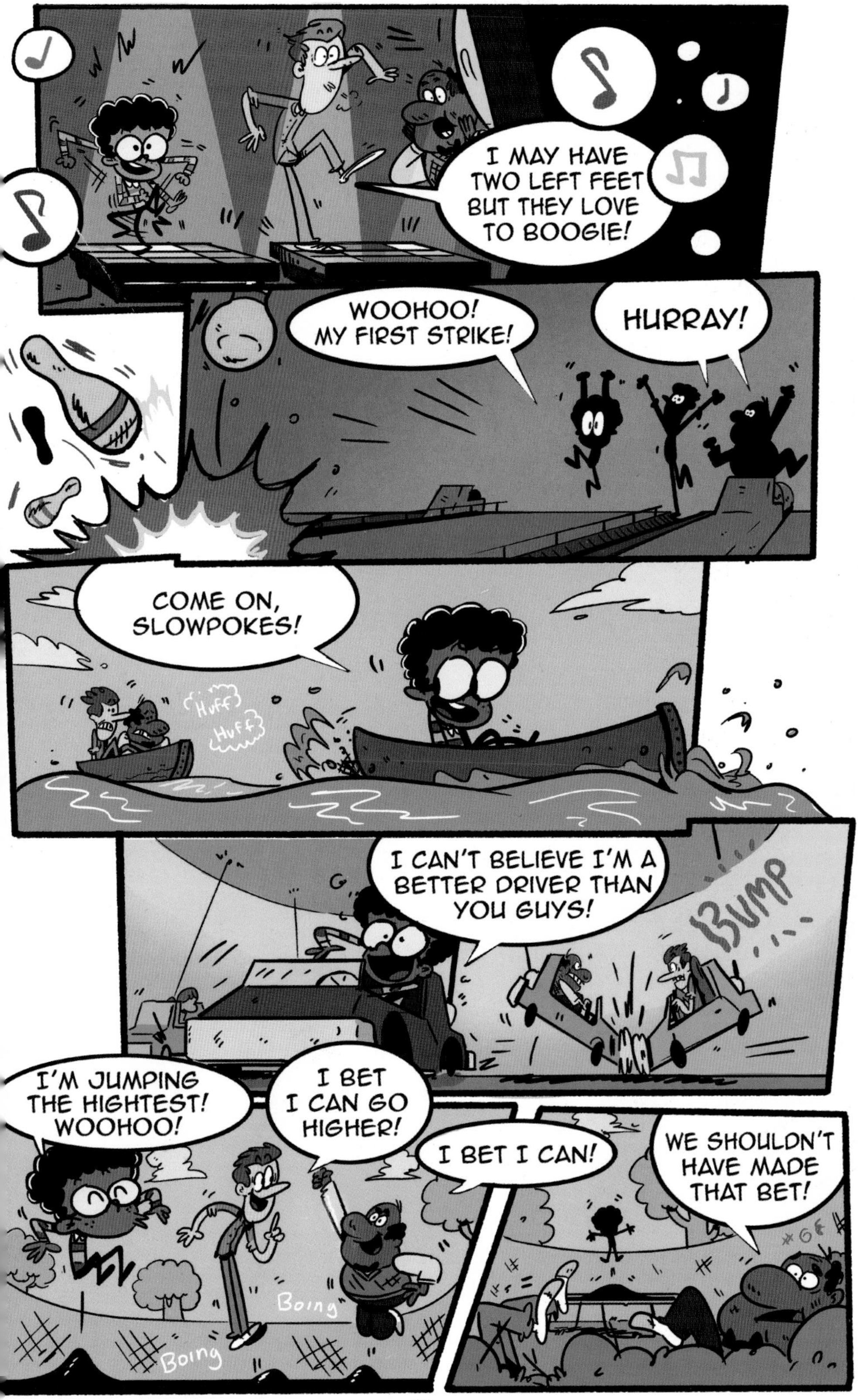
I MAY HAVE TWO LEFT FEET BUT THEY LOVE TO BOOGIE!
WOOHOO! MY FIRST STRIKE!
HURRAY!
COME ON, SLOWPOKES!
Huff
Huff
I CAN'T BELIEVE I'M A BETTER DRIVER THAN YOU GUYS!
BUMP
I'M JUMPING THE HIGHTEST! WOOHOO!
I BET I CAN GO HIGHER!
I BET I CAN!
Boing
Boing
WE SHOULDN'T HAVE MADE THAT BET!

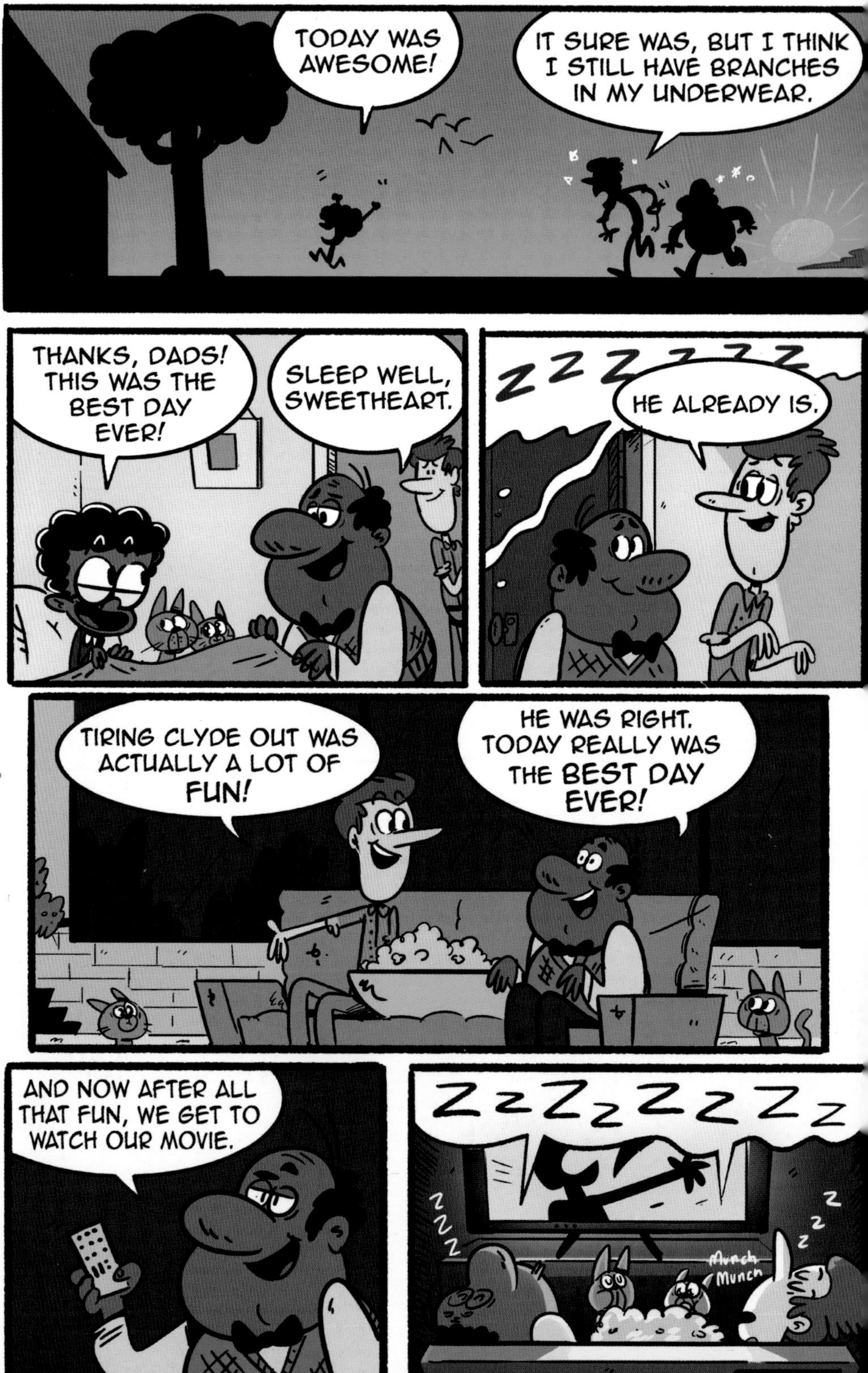
TODAY WAS AWESOME!
IT SURE WAS, BUT I THINK I STILL HAVE BRANCHES IN MY UNDERWEAR.
THANKS, DADS! THIS WAS THE BEST DAY EVER!
SLEEP WELL, SWEETHEART.
ZZZZZZZ
HE ALREADY IS.
TIRING CLYDE OUT WAS ACTUALLY A LOT OF FUN!
HE WAS RIGHT. TODAY REALLY WAS THE BEST DAY EVER!
AND NOW AFTER ALL THAT FUN, WE GET TO WATCH OUR MOVIE.
ZzZzZZZz
ZZZ
ZZZ
Munch Munch
END

"LIGHTS OUT"

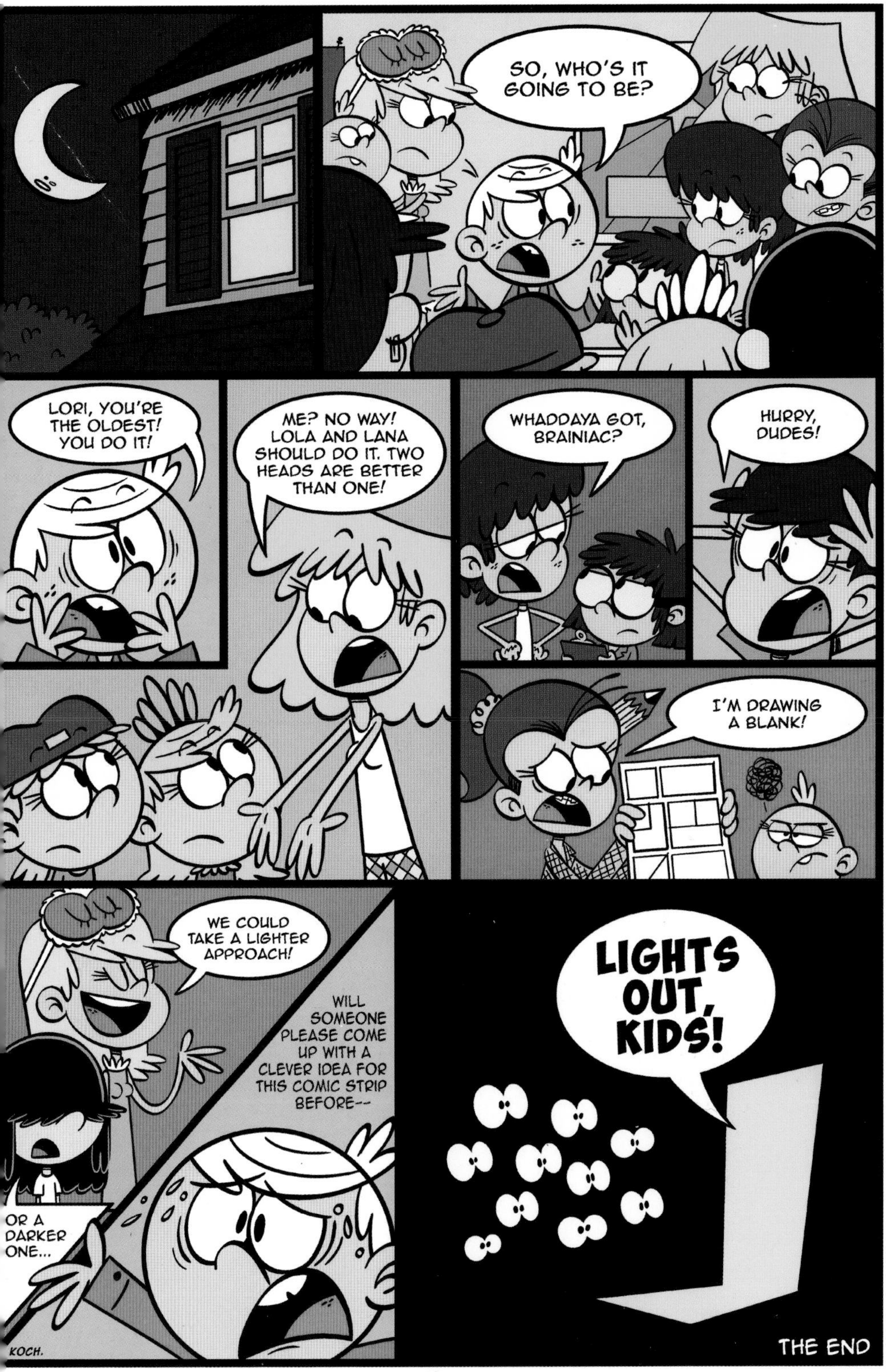
SO, WHO'S IT GOING TO BE?
LORI, YOU'RE THE OLDEST! YOU DO IT!
ME? NO WAY! LOLA AND LANA SHOULD DO IT. TWO HEADS ARE BETTER THAN ONE!
WHADDAYA GOT, BRAINIAC?
HURRY, DUDES!
I'M DRAWING A BLANK!
WE COULD TAKE A LIGHTER APPROACH!
OR A DARKER ONE...
WILL SOMEONE PLEASE COME UP WITH A CLEVER IDEA FOR THIS COMIC STRIP BEFORE--
LIGHTS OUT, KIDS!
THE END
KOCH.

"THE 10-HEADED BEAST"

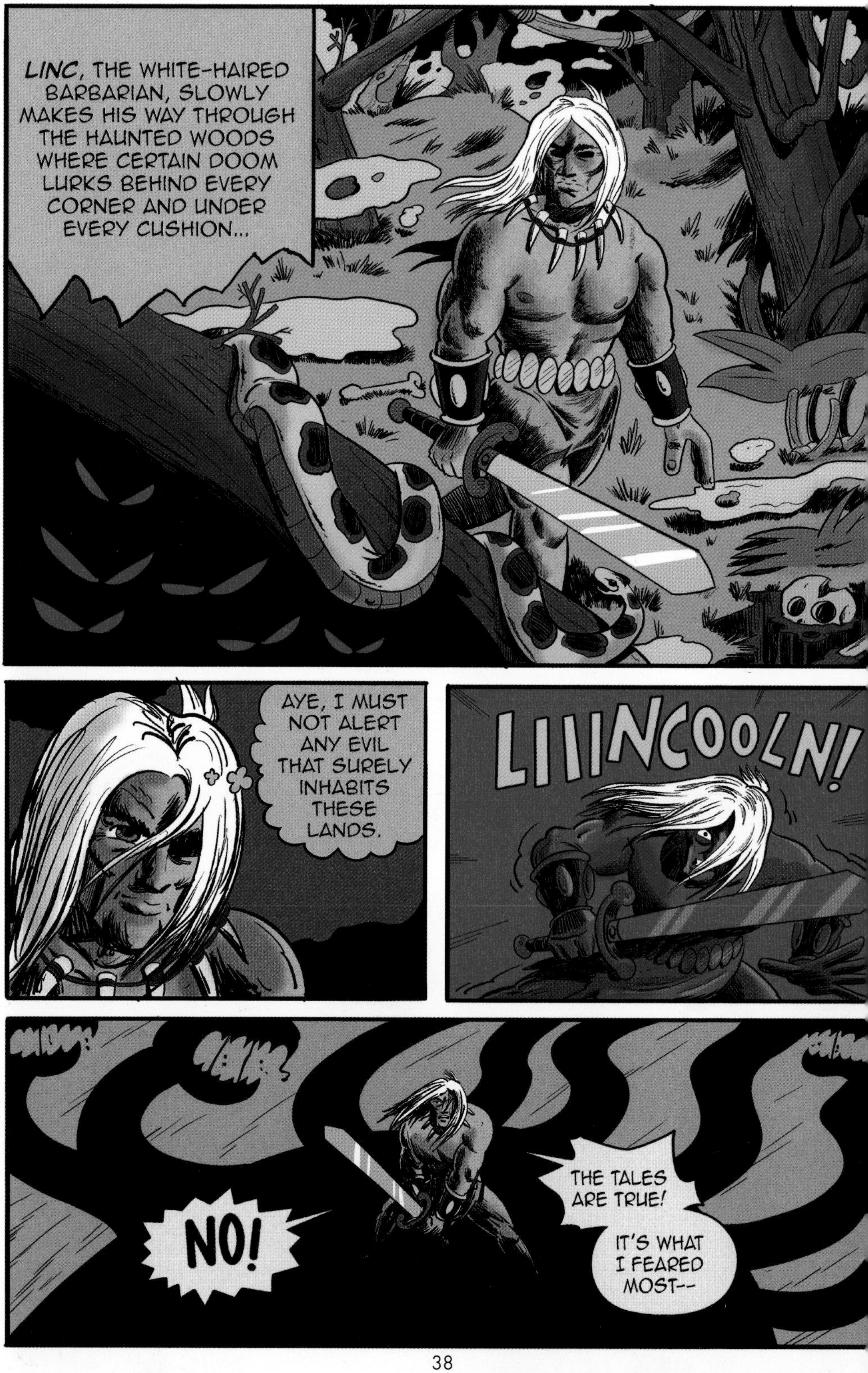
LINC, THE WHITE-HAIRED BARBARIAN, SLOWLY MAKES HIS WAY THROUGH THE HAUNTED WOODS WHERE CERTAIN DOOM LURKS BEHIND EVERY CORNER AND UNDER EVERY CUSHION...
AYE, I MUST NOT ALERT ANY EVIL THAT SURELY INHABITS THESE LANDS.
LIIINCOOLN!
THE TALES ARE TRUE!
IT'S WHAT I FEARED MOST--
NO!

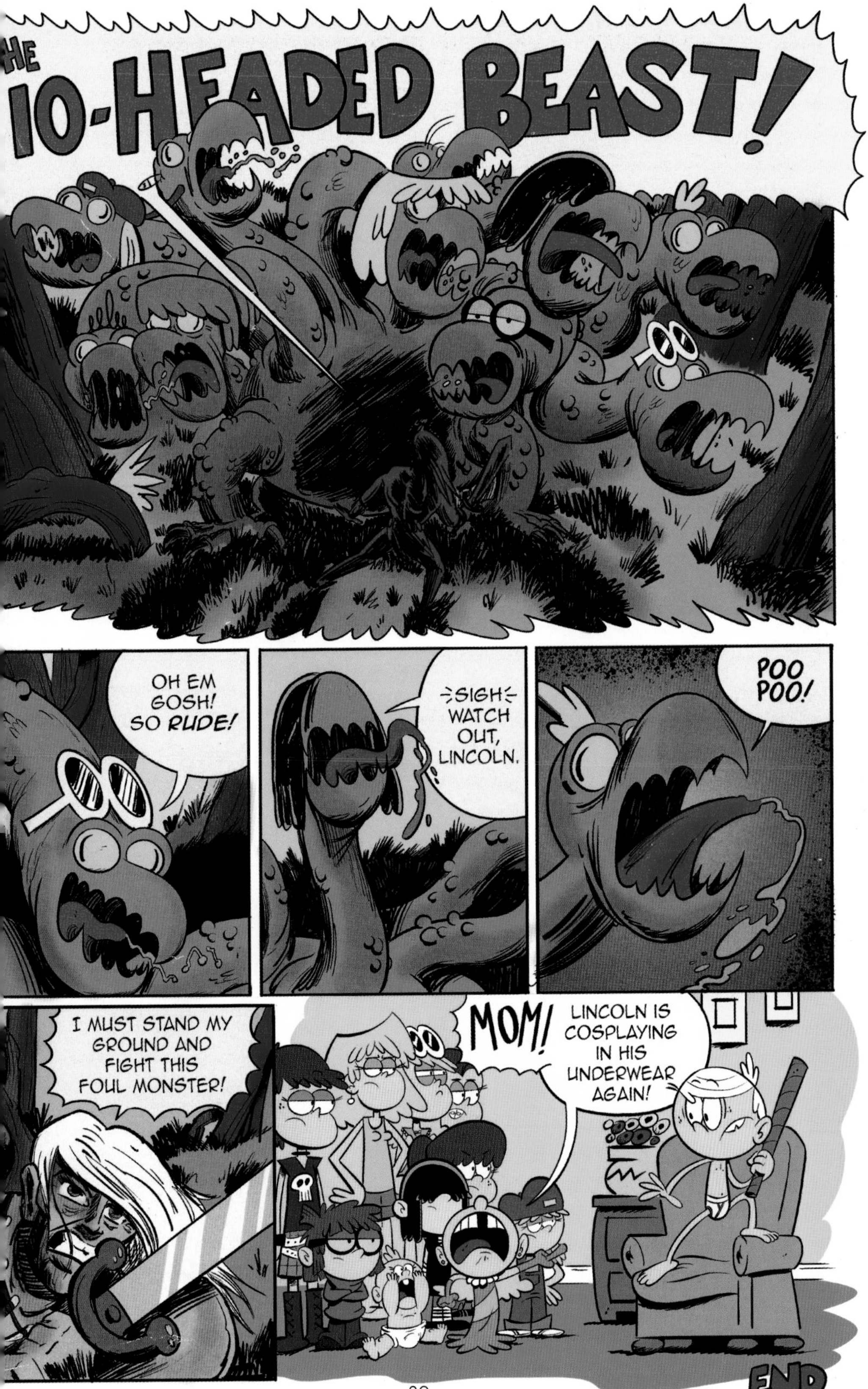
THE 10-HEADED BEAST!
OH EM GOSH! SO RUDE!
SIGH WATCH OUT, LINCOLN.
POO POO!
I MUST STAND MY GROUND AND FIGHT THIS FOUL MONSTER!
MOM!
LINCOLN IS COSPLAYING IN HIS UNDERWEAR AGAIN!
END

"TRAFFIC JAM"

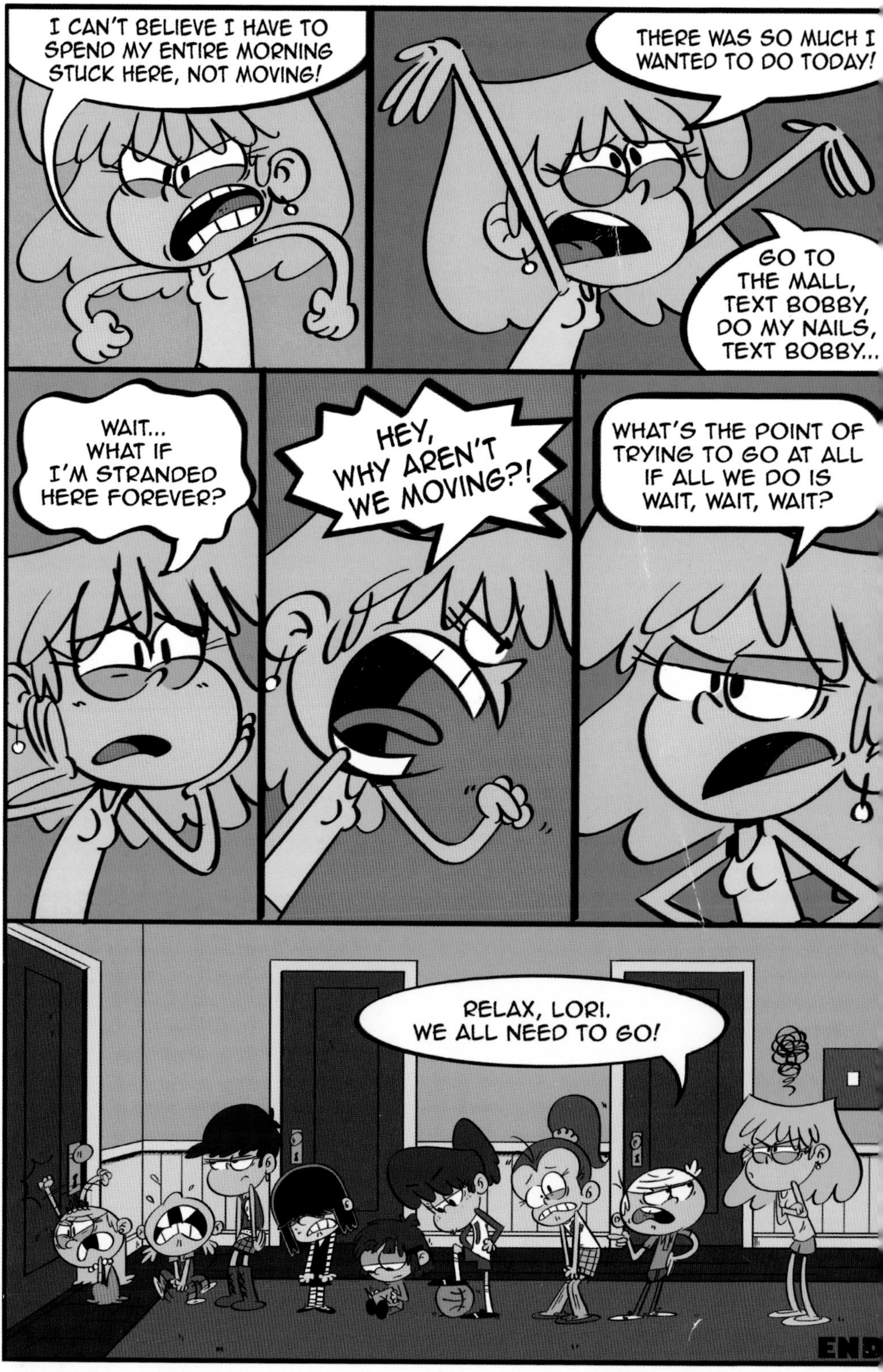
I CAN'T BELIEVE I HAVE TO SPEND MY ENTIRE MORNING STUCK HERE, NOT MOVING!
THERE WAS SO MUCH I WANTED TO DO TODAY!
GO TO THE MALL, TEXT BOBBY, DO MY NAILS, TEXT BOBBY...
WAIT... WHAT IF I'M STRANDED HERE FOREVER?
HEY, WHY AREN'T WE MOVING?!
WHAT'S THE POINT OF TRYING TO GO AT ALL IF ALL WE DO IS WAIT, WAIT, WAIT?
RELAX, LORI. WE ALL NEED TO GO!
END

"BAGGED AND BOARDED"

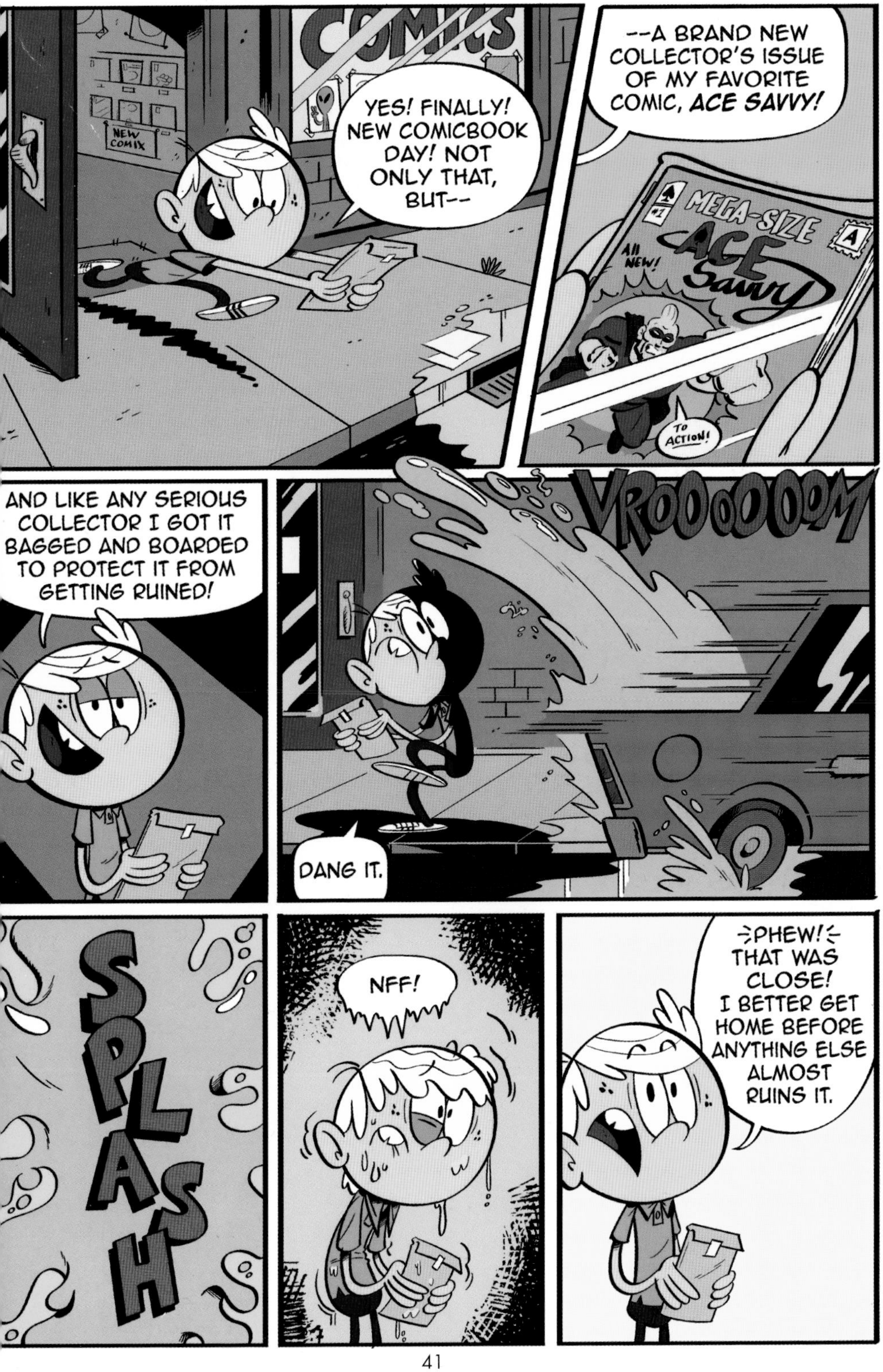

COMICS
NEW COMIX
YES! FINALLY! NEW COMICBOOK DAY! NOT ONLY THAT, BUT--
--A BRAND NEW COLLECTOR'S ISSUE OF MY FAVORITE COMIC, ACE SAVVY!
MEGA-SIZE ACE Savvy
#1
All NEW!
TO ACTION!
AND LIKE ANY SERIOUS COLLECTOR I GOT IT BAGGED AND BOARDED TO PROTECT IT FROM GETTING RUINED!
VROOOOOOM
DANG IT.
SPLASH
NFF!
PHEW! THAT WAS CLOSE! I BETTER GET HOME BEFORE ANYTHING ELSE ALMOST RUINS IT.

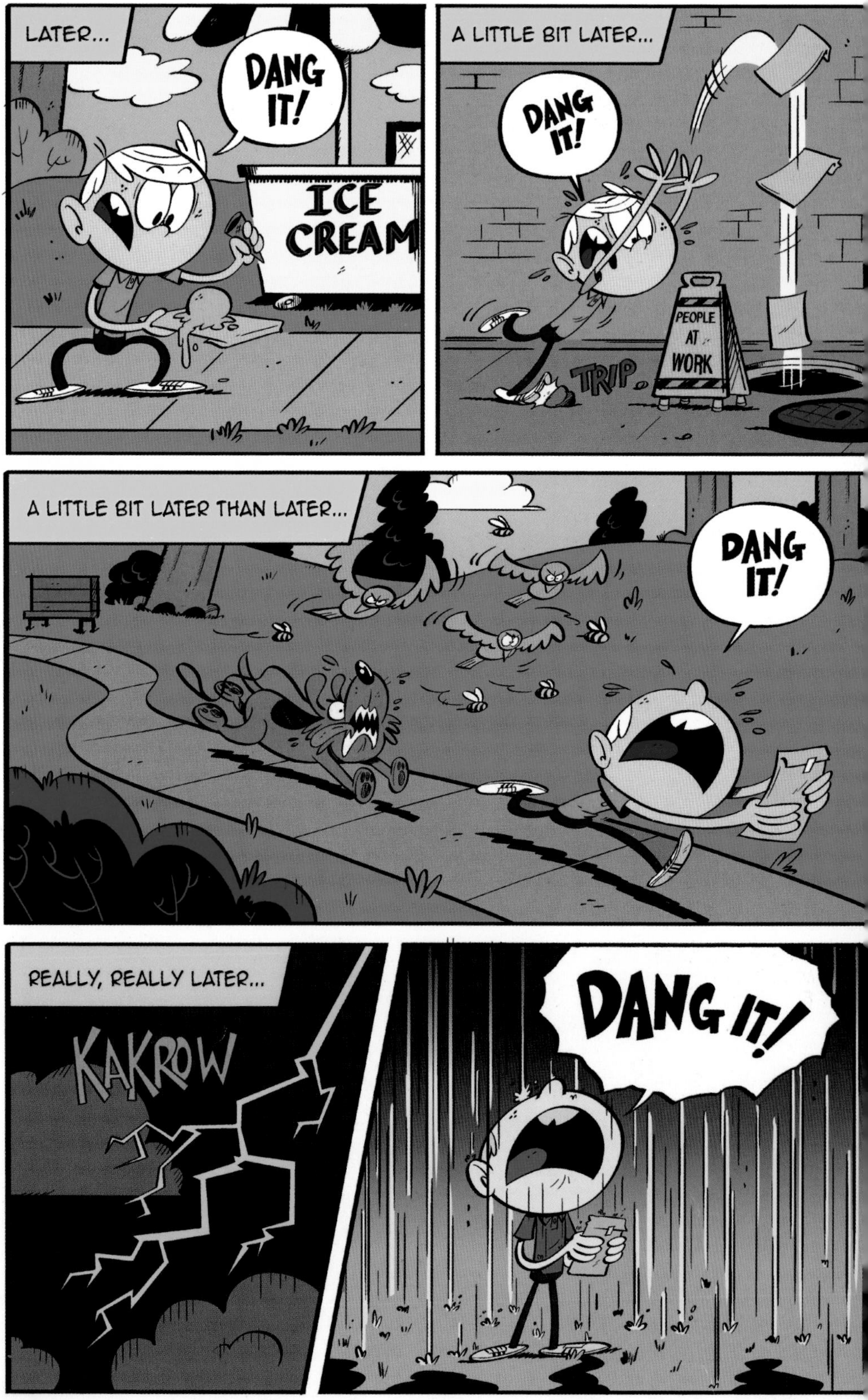
LATER...
DANG IT!
ICE CREAM
A LITTLE BIT LATER...
DANG IT!
PEOPLE AT WORK
TRIP
A LITTLE BIT LATER THAN LATER...
DANG IT!
REALLY, REALLY LATER...
KAKROW
DANG IT!

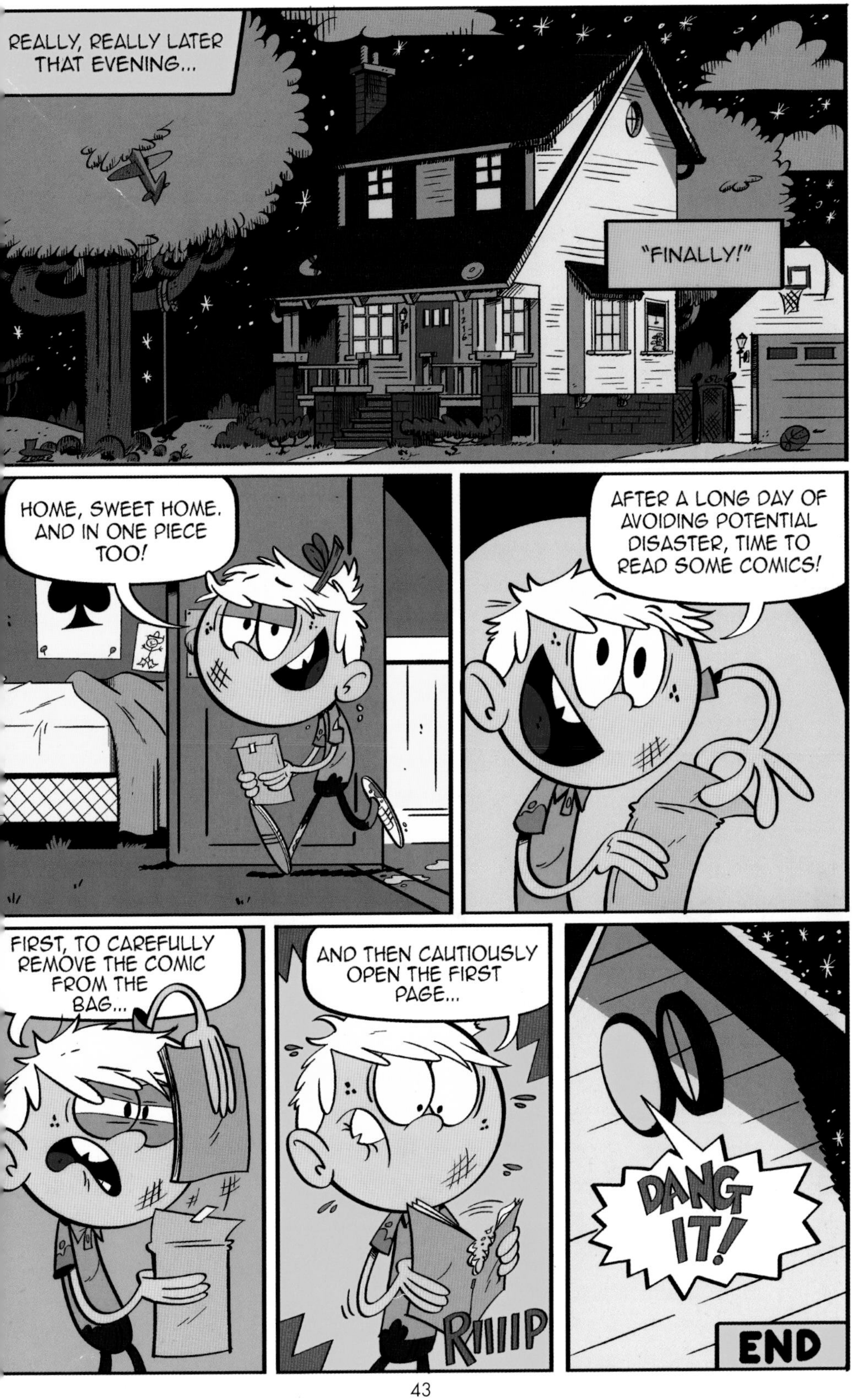
REALLY, REALLY LATER THAT EVENING...
"FINALLY!"
HOME, SWEET HOME. AND IN ONE PIECE TOO!
AFTER A LONG DAY OF AVOIDING POTENTIAL DISASTER, TIME TO READ SOME COMICS!
FIRST, TO CAREFULLY REMOVE THE COMIC FROM THE BAG...
AND THEN CAUTIOUSLY OPEN THE FIRST PAGE...
RIIIIP
DANG IT!
END

"SHOE STYLIN'"

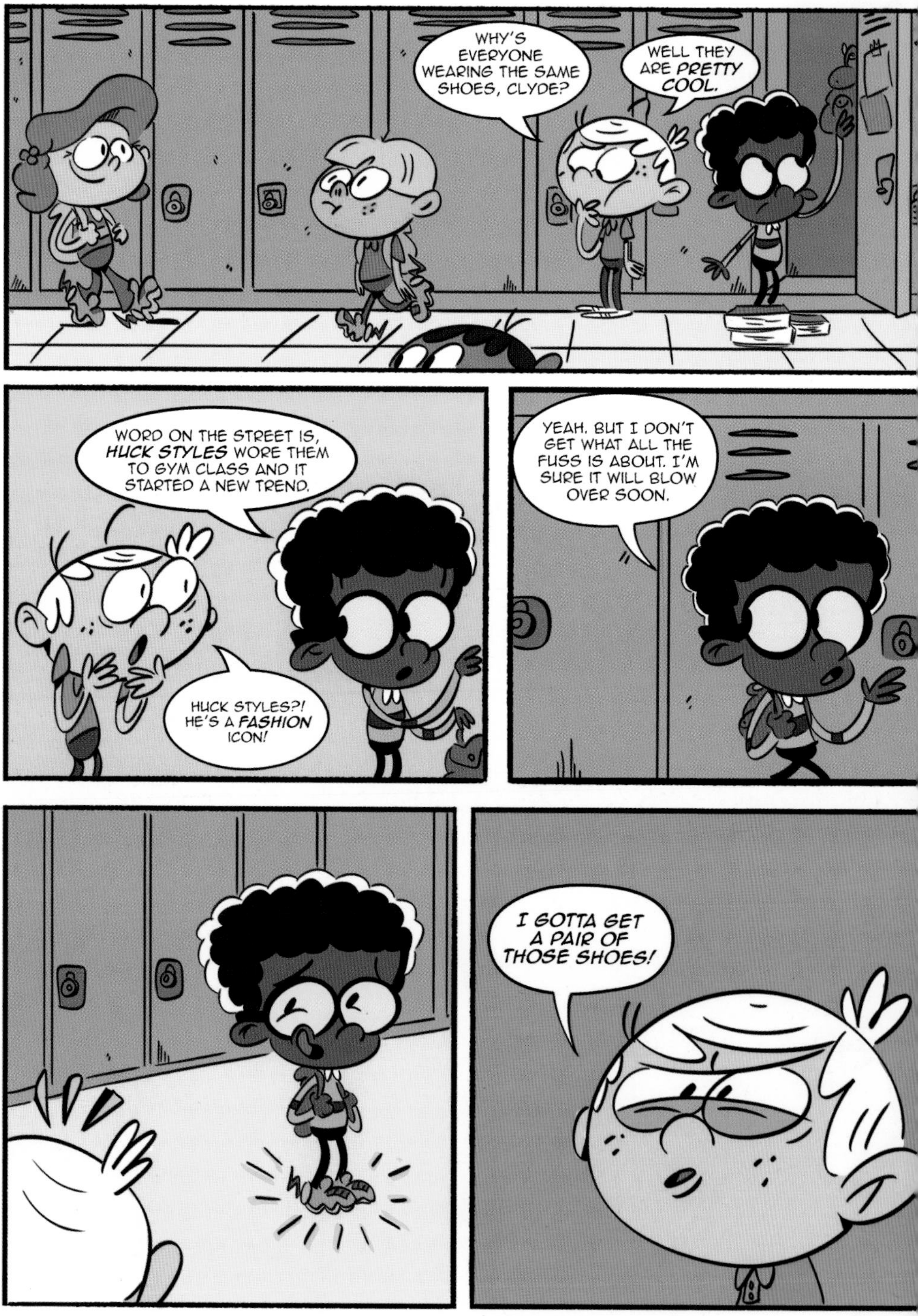
WHY'S EVERYONE WEARING THE SAME SHOES, CLYDE?
WELL THEY ARE PRETTY COOL.
WORD ON THE STREET IS, HUCK STYLES WORE THEM TO GYM CLASS AND IT STARTED A NEW TREND.
HUCK STYLES?! HE'S A FASHION ICON!
YEAH. BUT I DON'T GET WHAT ALL THE FUSS IS ABOUT. I'M SURE IT WILL BLOW OVER SOON.
I GOTTA GET A PAIR OF THOSE SHOES!

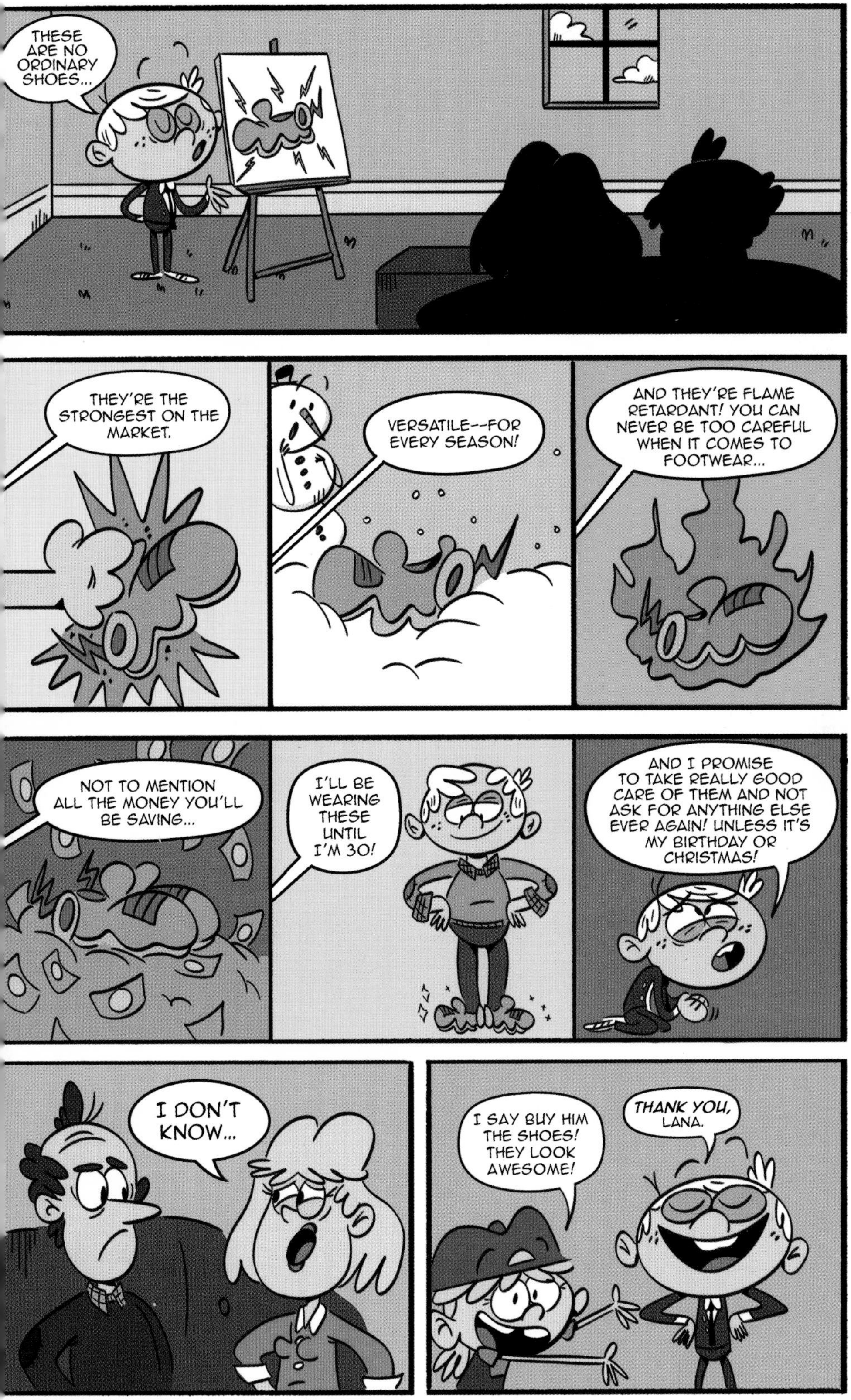
THESE ARE NO ORDINARY SHOES...
THEY'RE THE STRONGEST ON THE MARKET.
VERSATILE--FOR EVERY SEASON!
AND THEY'RE FLAME RETARDANT! YOU CAN NEVER BE TOO CAREFUL WHEN IT COMES TO FOOTWEAR...
NOT TO MENTION ALL THE MONEY YOU'LL BE SAVING...
I'LL BE WEARING THESE UNTIL I'M 30!
AND I PROMISE TO TAKE REALLY GOOD CARE OF THEM AND NOT ASK FOR ANYTHING ELSE EVER AGAIN! UNLESS IT'S MY BIRTHDAY OR CHRISTMAS!
I DON'T KNOW...
I SAY BUY HIM THE SHOES! THEY LOOK AWESOME!
THANK YOU, LANA.

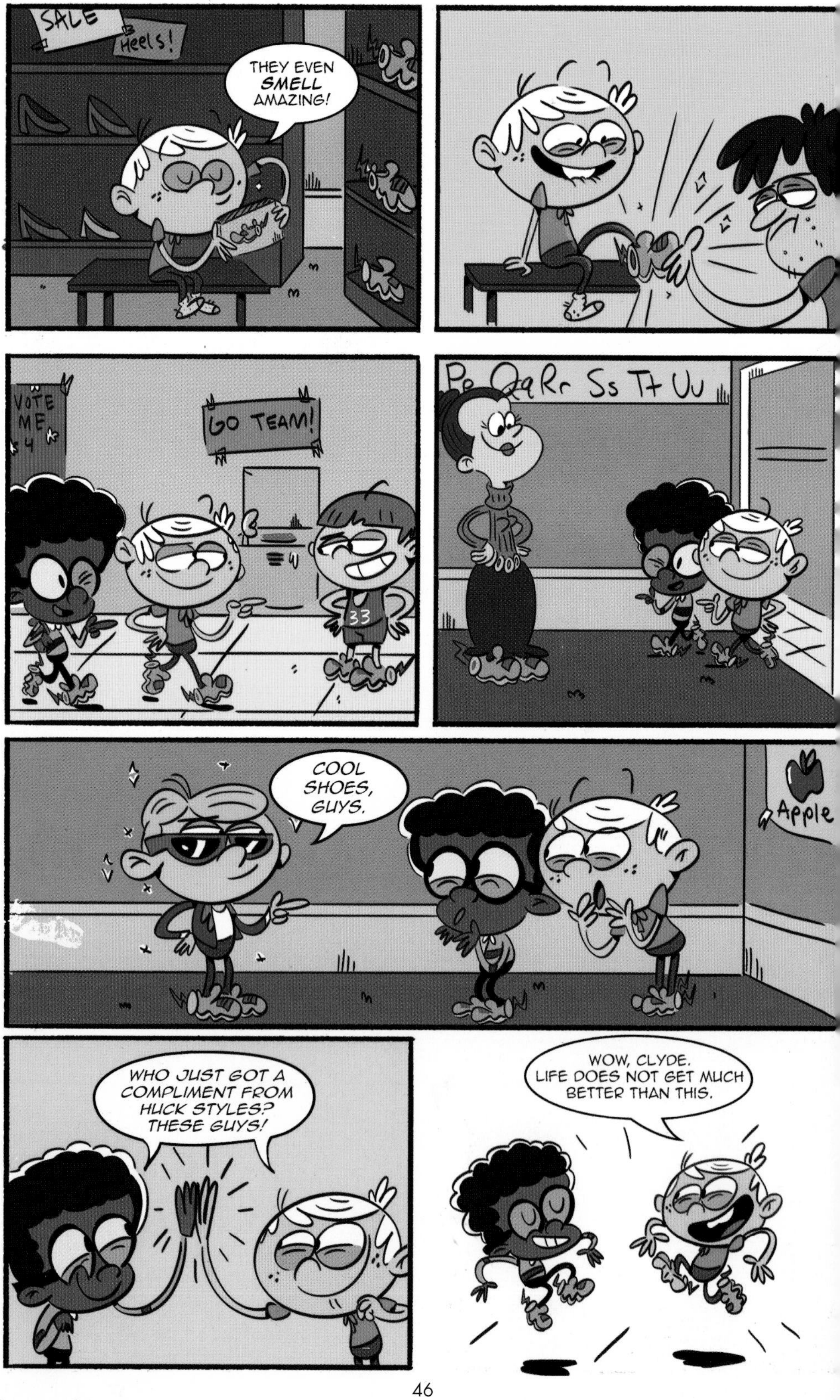
SALE
Heels!
THEY EVEN SMELL AMAZING!
VOTE ME 4
GO TEAM!
33
Pp Qq Rr Ss Tt Uu
COOL SHOES, GUYS.
Apple
WHO JUST GOT A COMPLIMENT FROM HUCK STYLES? THESE GUYS!
WOW, CLYDE. LIFE DOES NOT GET MUCH BETTER THAN THIS.

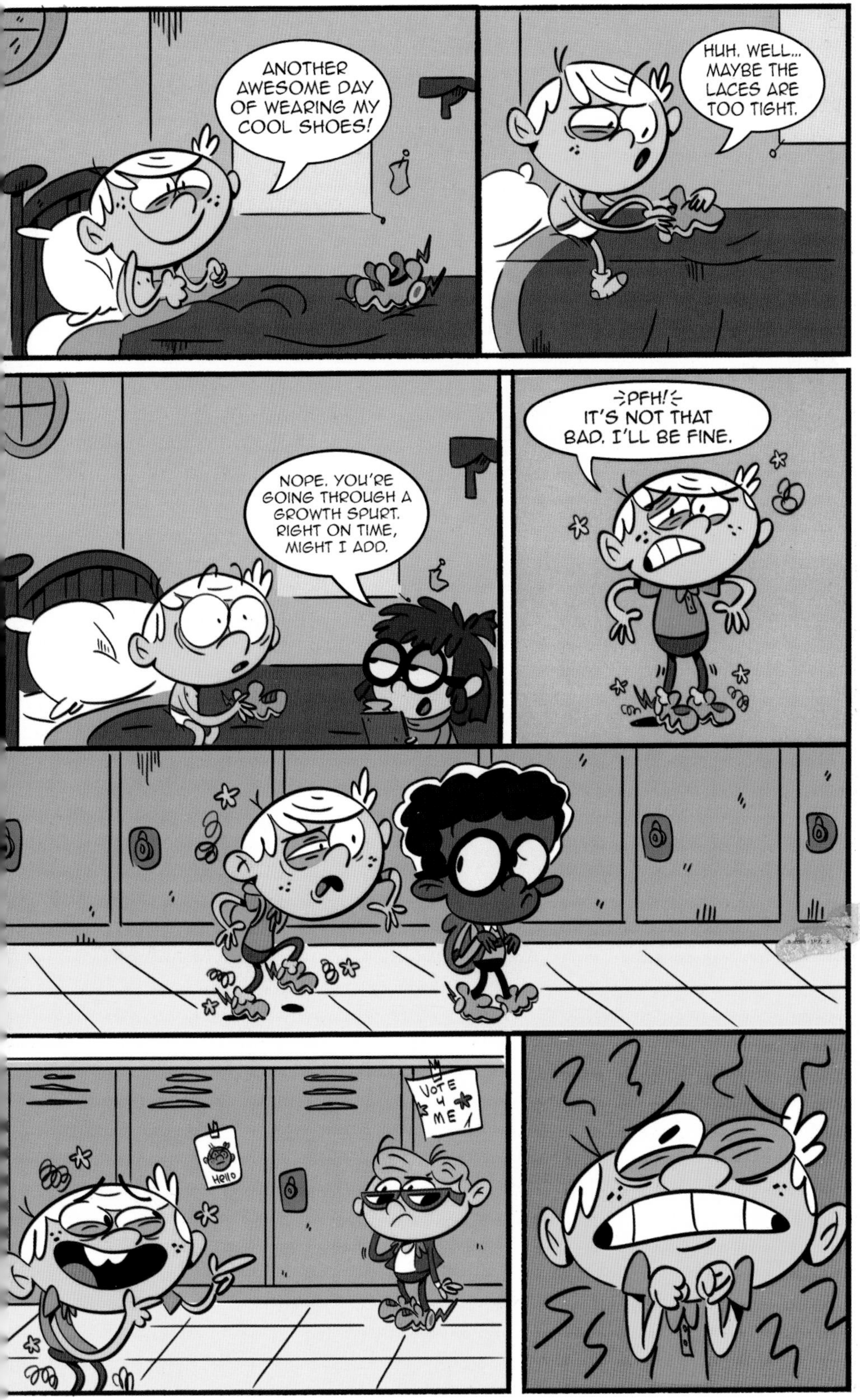
ANOTHER AWESOME DAY OF WEARING MY COOL SHOES!
HUH. WELL... MAYBE THE LACES ARE TOO TIGHT.
NOPE. YOU'RE GOING THROUGH A GROWTH SPURT. RIGHT ON TIME, MIGHT I ADD.
PFH! IT'S NOT THAT BAD. I'LL BE FINE.
VOTE 4 ME
Hello

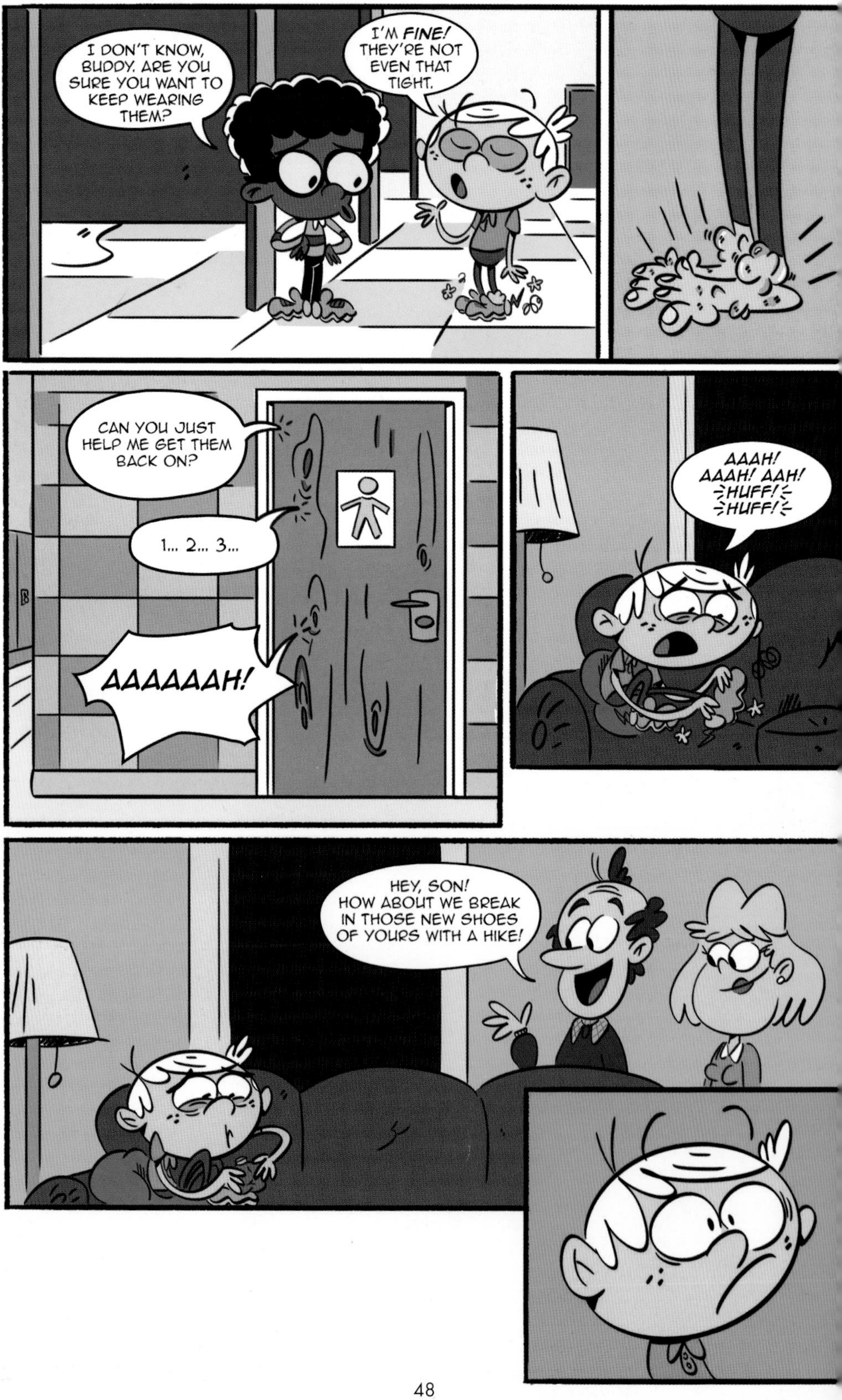
I DON'T KNOW, BUDDY. ARE YOU SURE YOU WANT TO KEEP WEARING THEM?
I'M FINE! THEY'RE NOT EVEN THAT TIGHT.
CAN YOU JUST HELP ME GET THEM BACK ON?
1... 2... 3...
AAAAAAH!
AAAH! AAAH! AAH! HUFF! HUFF!
HEY, SON! HOW ABOUT WE BREAK IN THOSE NEW SHOES OF YOURS WITH A HIKE!

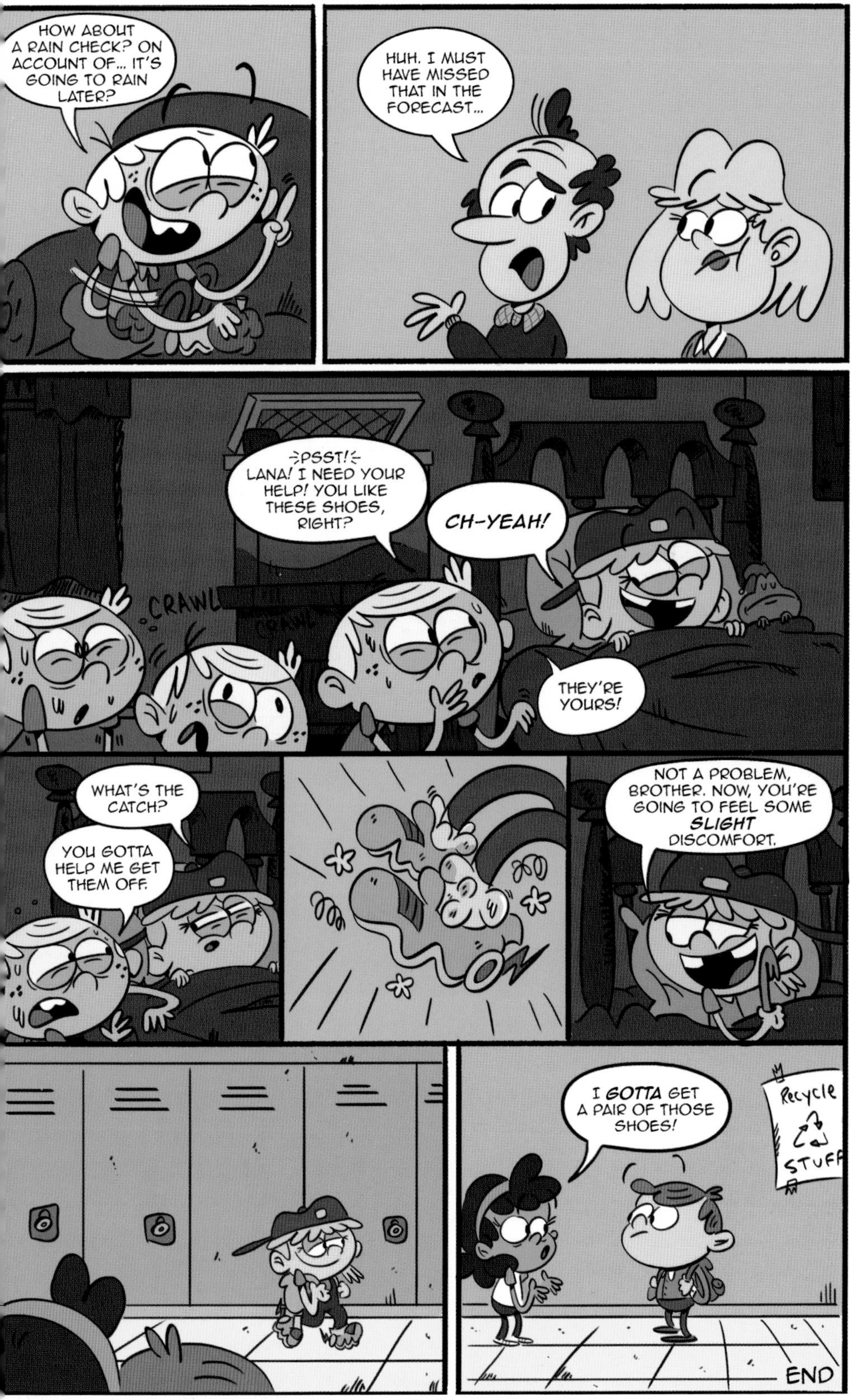
HOW ABOUT A RAIN CHECK? ON ACCOUNT OF... IT'S GOING TO RAIN LATER?
HUH. I MUST HAVE MISSED THAT IN THE FORECAST...
PSST! LANA! I NEED YOUR HELP! YOU LIKE THESE SHOES, RIGHT?
CH-YEAH!
CRAWL
CRAWL
THEY'RE YOURS!
WHAT'S THE CATCH?
YOU GOTTA HELP ME GET THEM OFF.
NOT A PROBLEM, BROTHER. NOW, YOU'RE GOING TO FEEL SOME SLIGHT DISCOMFORT.
I GOTTA GET A PAIR OF THOSE SHOES!
Recycle STUFF
END

"THE ART OF COOKING"

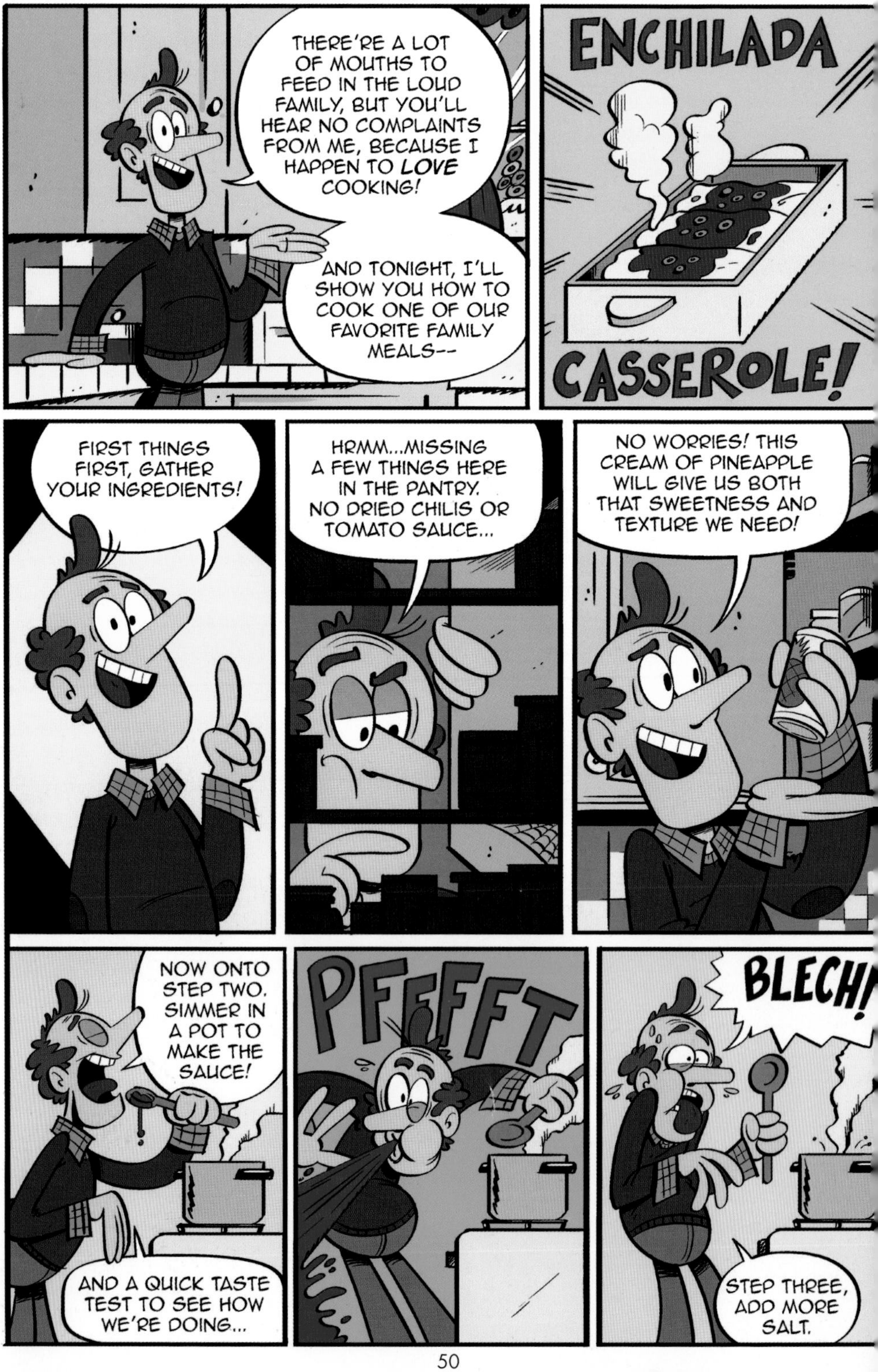

THERE'RE A LOT OF MOUTHS TO FEED IN THE LOUD FAMILY, BUT YOU'LL HEAR NO COMPLAINTS FROM ME, BECAUSE I HAPPEN TO *LOVE* COOKING!
AND TONIGHT, I'LL SHOW YOU HOW TO COOK ONE OF OUR FAVORITE FAMILY MEALS--
ENCHILADA CASSEROLE!
FIRST THINGS FIRST, GATHER YOUR INGREDIENTS!
HRMM...MISSING A FEW THINGS HERE IN THE PANTRY. NO DRIED CHILIS OR TOMATO SAUCE...
NO WORRIES! THIS CREAM OF PINEAPPLE WILL GIVE US BOTH THAT SWEETNESS AND TEXTURE WE NEED!
NOW ONTO STEP TWO. SIMMER IN A POT TO MAKE THE SAUCE!
AND A QUICK TASTE TEST TO SEE HOW WE'RE DOING...
PFFFFT
BLECH!
STEP THREE, ADD MORE SALT.

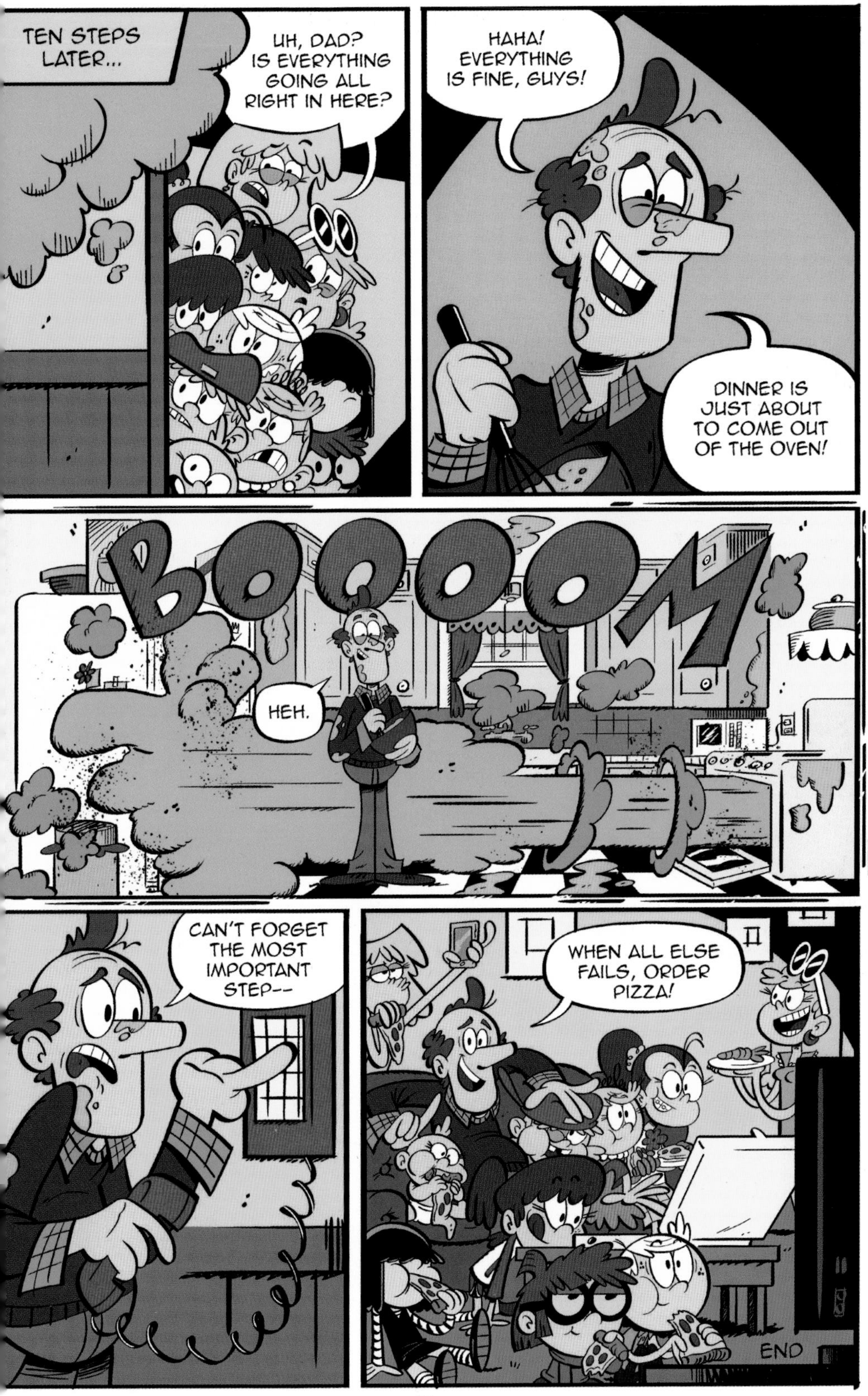
TEN STEPS LATER...
UH, DAD? IS EVERYTHING GOING ALL RIGHT IN HERE?
HAHA! EVERYTHING IS FINE, GUYS!
DINNER IS JUST ABOUT TO COME OUT OF THE OVEN!
BOOOOM
HEH.
CAN'T FORGET THE MOST IMPORTANT STEP--
WHEN ALL ELSE FAILS, ORDER PIZZA!
END

"THE BORROWERS"

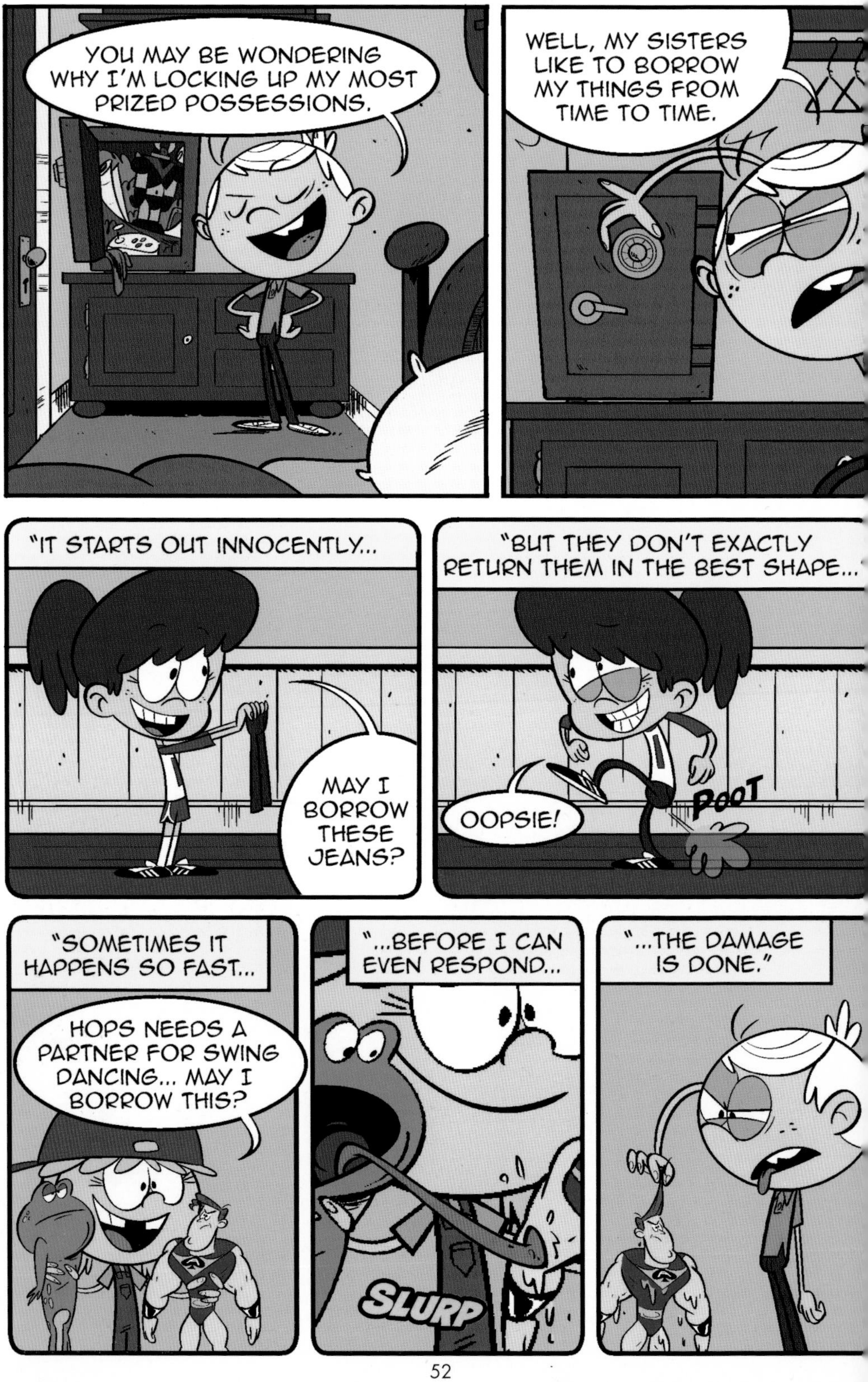

YOU MAY BE WONDERING WHY I'M LOCKING UP MY MOST PRIZED POSSESSIONS.
WELL, MY SISTERS LIKE TO BORROW MY THINGS FROM TIME TO TIME.
"IT STARTS OUT INNOCENTLY...
MAY I BORROW THESE JEANS?
"BUT THEY DON'T EXACTLY RETURN THEM IN THE BEST SHAPE...
OOPSIE!
POOT
"SOMETIMES IT HAPPENS SO FAST...
HOPS NEEDS A PARTNER FOR SWING DANCING... MAY I BORROW THIS?
"...BEFORE I CAN EVEN RESPOND...
SLURP
"...THE DAMAGE IS DONE."

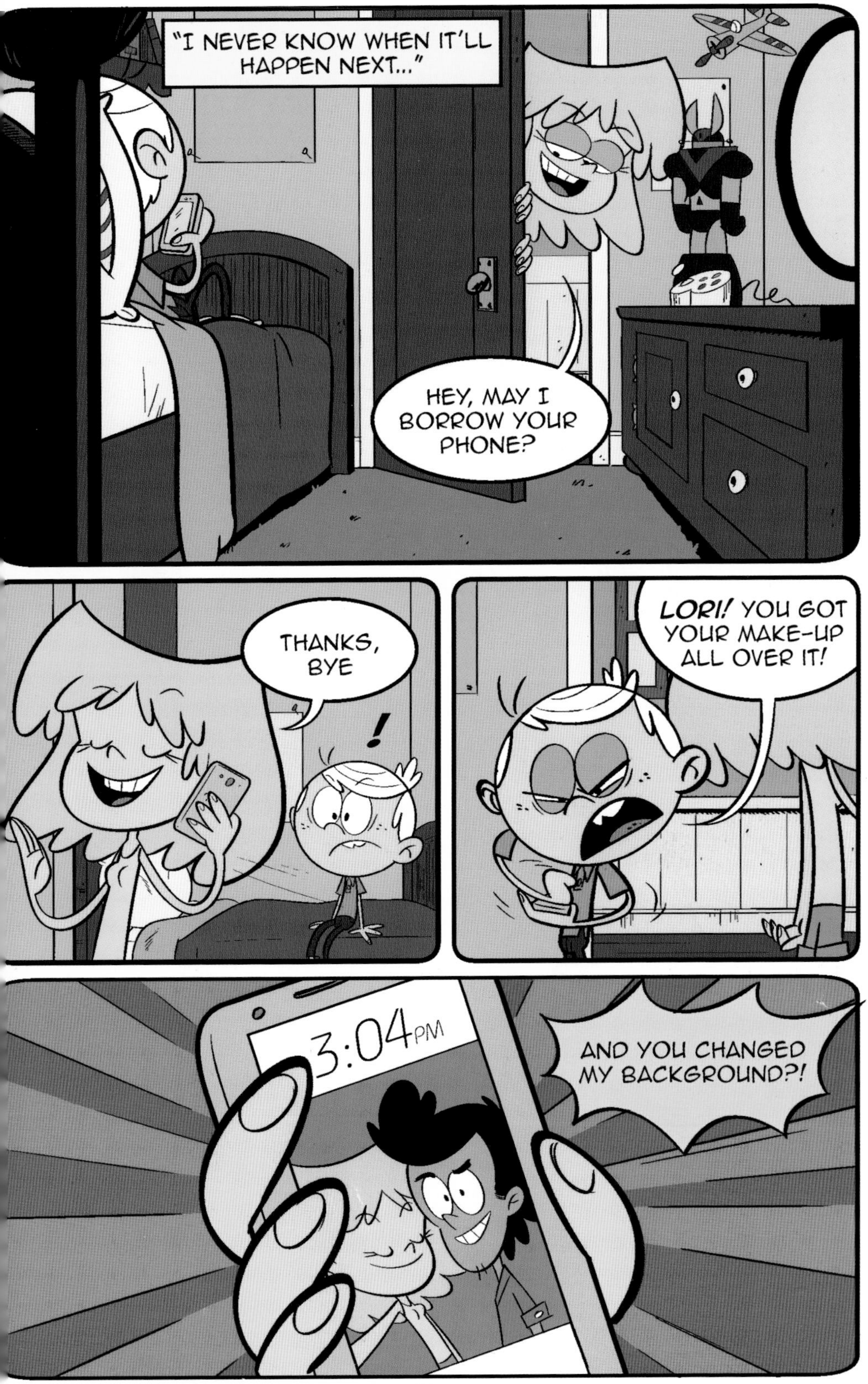
"I NEVER KNOW WHEN IT'LL HAPPEN NEXT..."
HEY, MAY I BORROW YOUR PHONE?
THANKS, BYE
!
LORI! YOU GOT YOUR MAKE-UP ALL OVER IT!
3:04PM
AND YOU CHANGED MY BACKGROUND?!

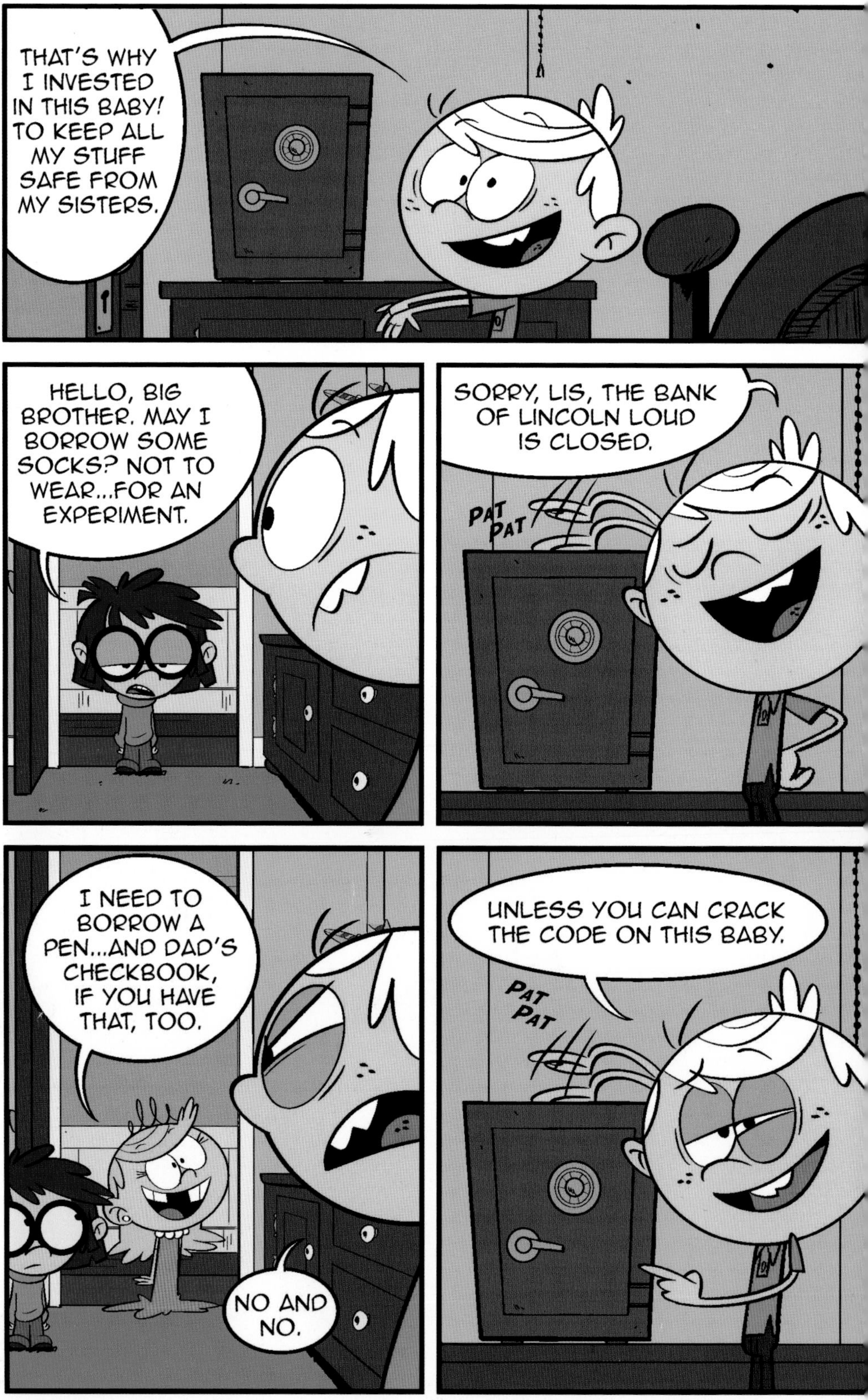
THAT'S WHY I INVESTED IN THIS BABY! TO KEEP ALL MY STUFF SAFE FROM MY SISTERS.
HELLO, BIG BROTHER. MAY I BORROW SOME SOCKS? NOT TO WEAR...FOR AN EXPERIMENT.
SORRY, LIS, THE BANK OF LINCOLN LOUD IS CLOSED.
PAT PAT
I NEED TO BORROW A PEN...AND DAD'S CHECKBOOK, IF YOU HAVE THAT, TOO.
NO AND NO.
UNLESS YOU CAN CRACK THE CODE ON THIS BABY.
PAT PAT

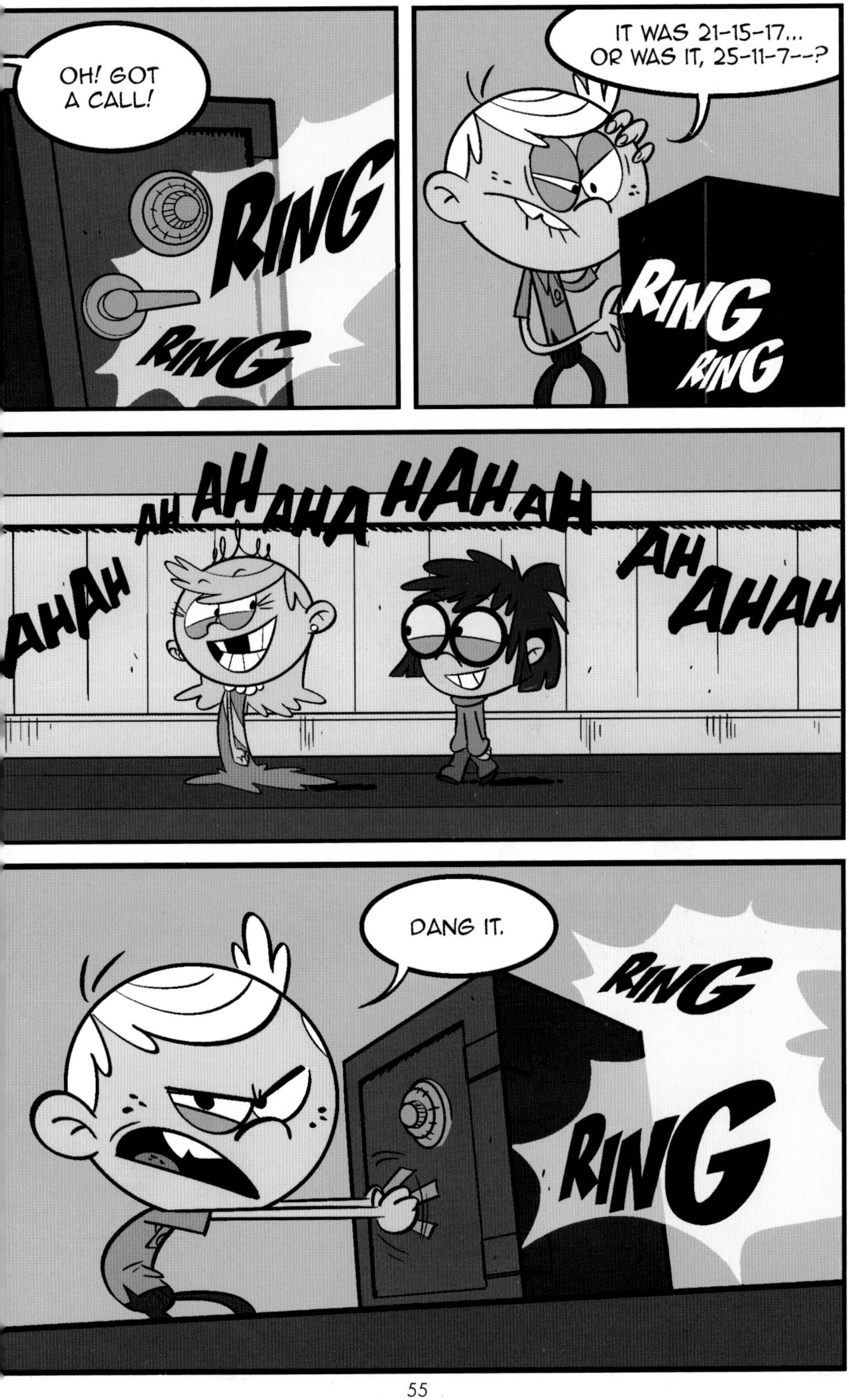
OH! GOT A CALL!
RING
RING
IT WAS 21-15-17... OR WAS IT, 25-11-7--?
RING
RING
AHAH
AH
AH
AHA
HAH
AH
AH
AH
AHAH
DANG IT.
RING
RING

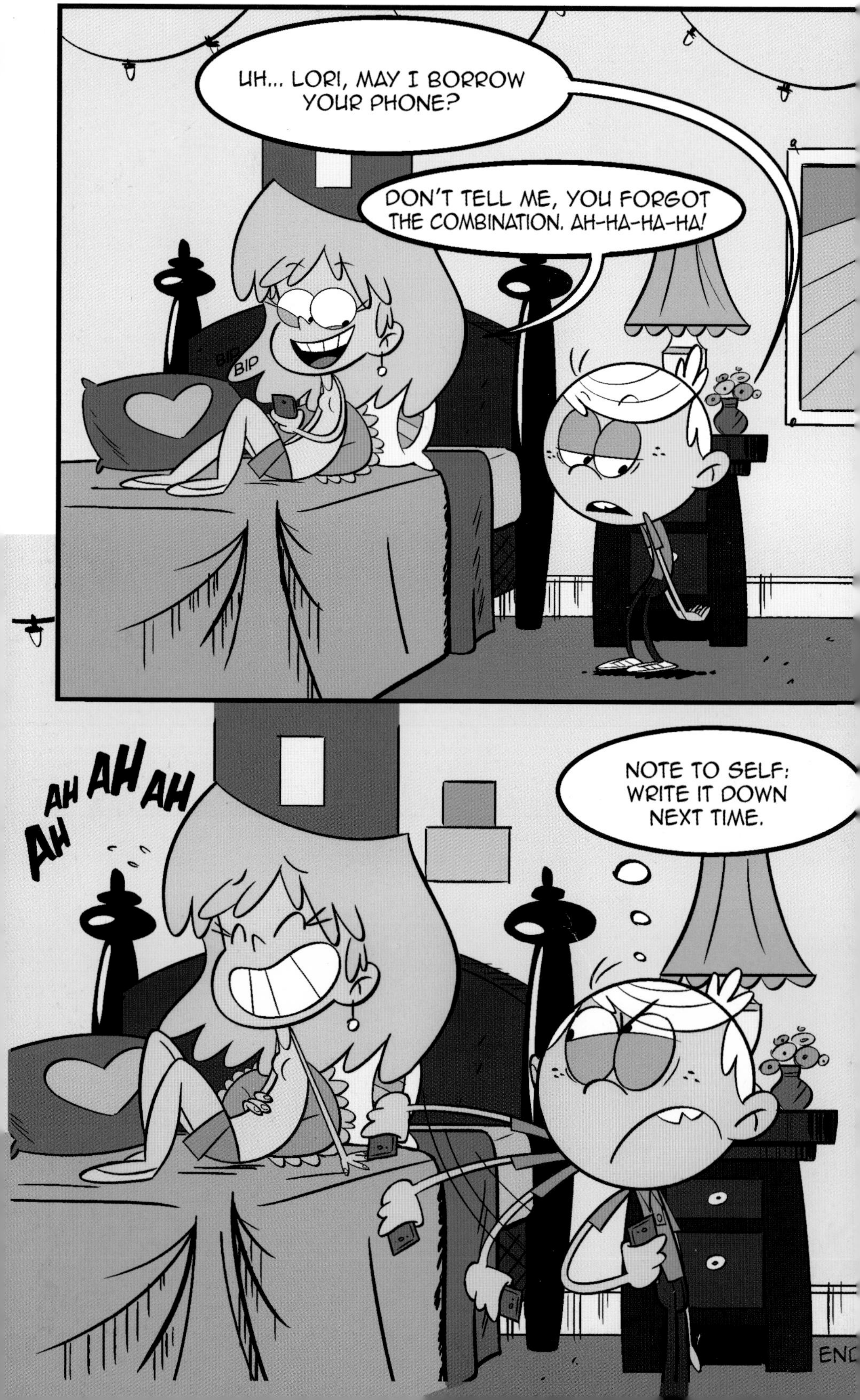
UH... LORI, MAY I BORROW YOUR PHONE?
DON'T TELL ME, YOU FORGOT THE COMBINATION. AH-HA-HA-HA!
BIP BIP
AH AH AH AH
NOTE TO SELF: WRITE IT DOWN NEXT TIME.
END

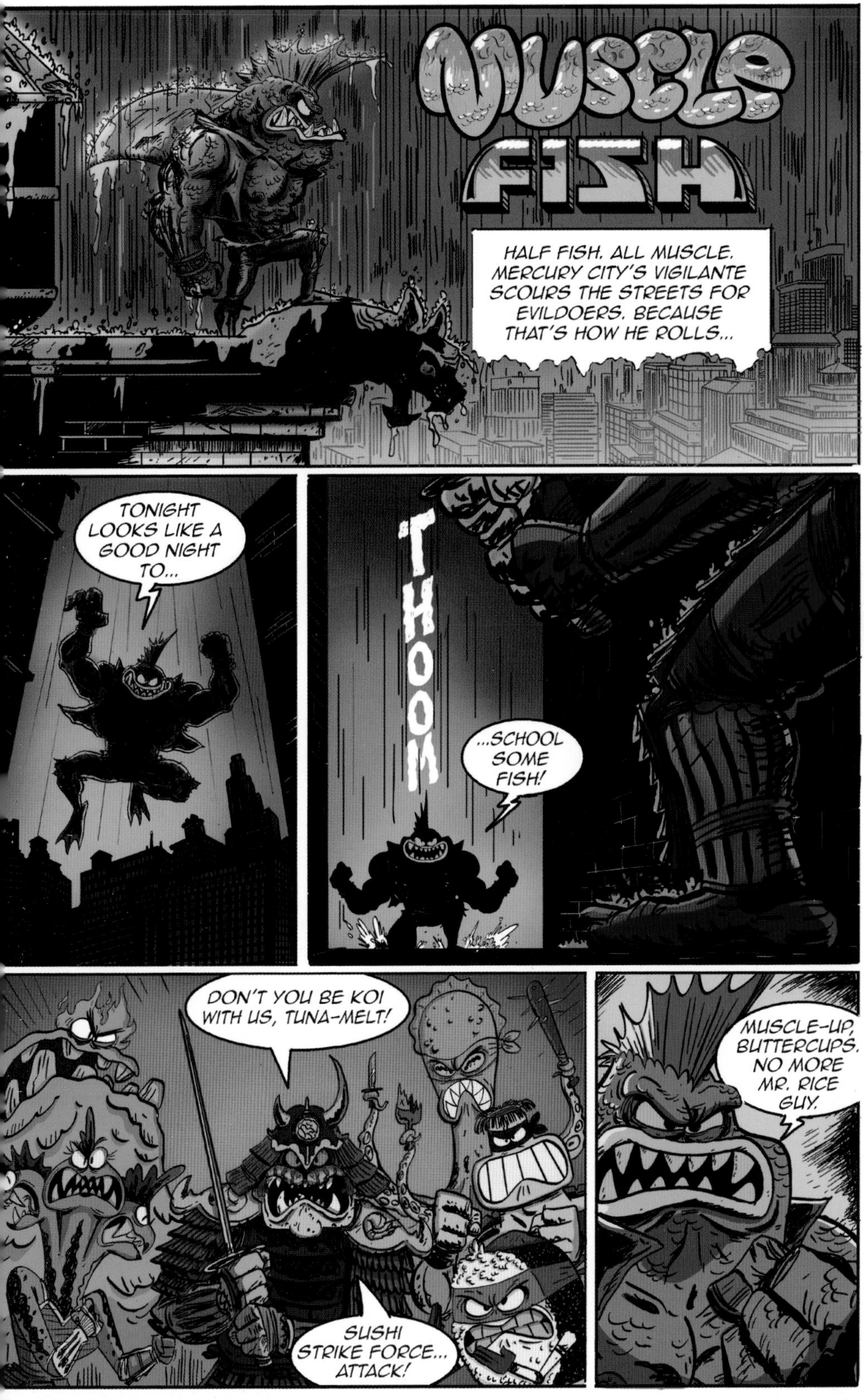
MUSCLE FISH
HALF FISH. ALL MUSCLE. MERCURY CITY'S VIGILANTE SCOURS THE STREETS FOR EVILDOERS. BECAUSE THAT'S HOW HE ROLLS...
TONIGHT LOOKS LIKE A GOOD NIGHT TO...
THOOM
...SCHOOL SOME FISH!
DON'T YOU BE KOI WITH US, TUNA-MELT!
SUSHI STRIKE FORCE... ATTACK!
MUSCLE-UP, BUTTERCUPS. NO MORE MR. RICE GUY.

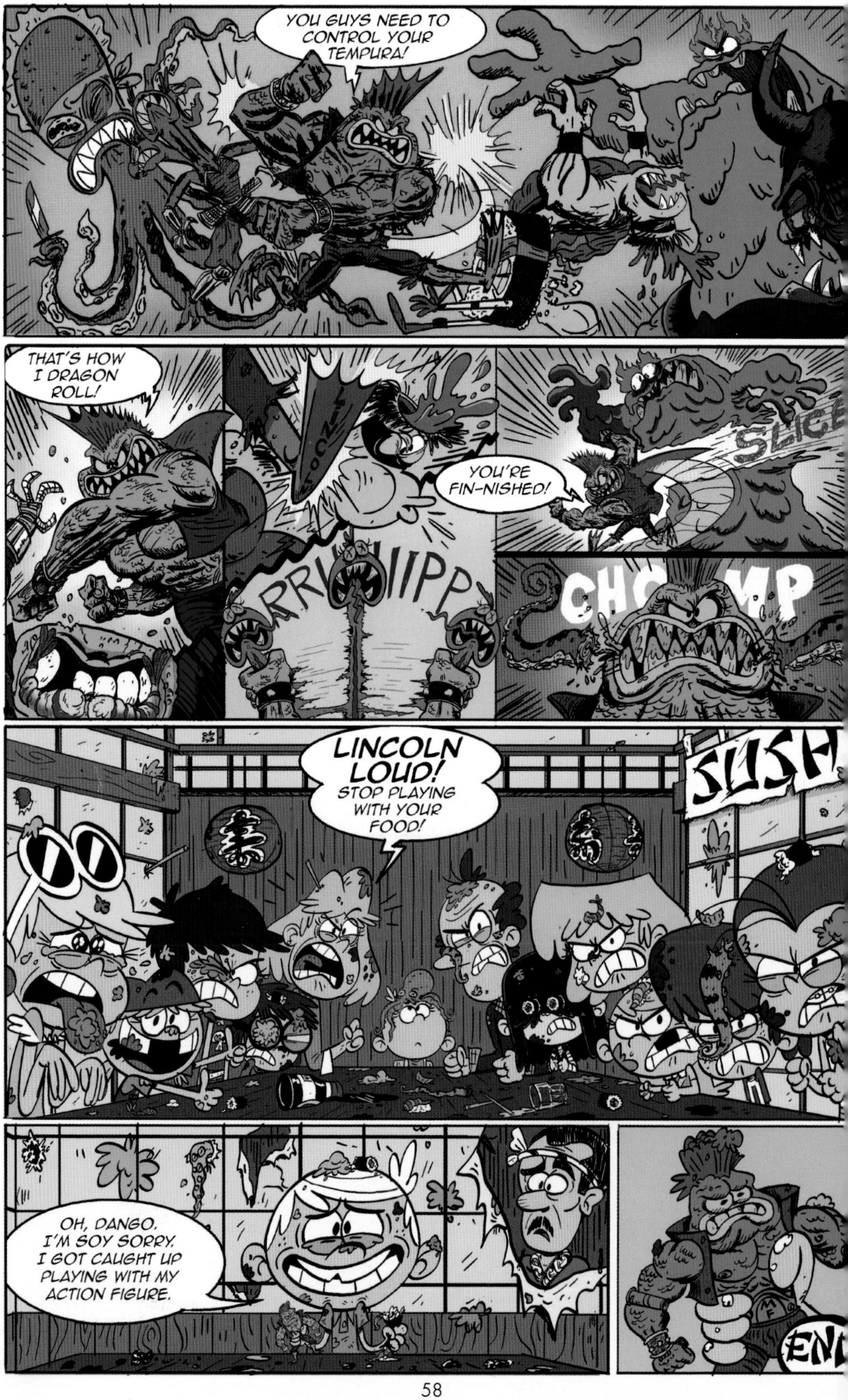

YOU GUYS NEED TO CONTROL YOUR TEMPURA!
THAT'S HOW I DRAGON ROLL!
YOU'RE FIN-NISHED!
SLICE
RRIIIIPP
CHOMP
LINCOLN LOUD! STOP PLAYING WITH YOUR FOOD!
SUSH
OH, DANGO. I'M SOY SORRY. I GOT CAUGHT UP PLAYING WITH MY ACTION FIGURE.

WATCH OUT FOR PAPERCUTZ

elcome to the second, sister-saturated *THE LOUD HOUSE* graphic novel from Papercutz—those sometime ɔabbling comicbook-lovers dedicated to publishing great graphic novels for all ages. I'm Jim Salicrup, the itor-in-Chief and big-time ACE SAVVY fan, and I'm here to talk about how people actually read comics.

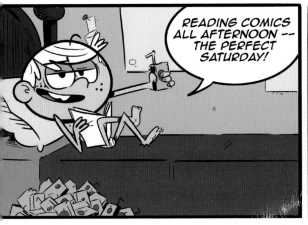

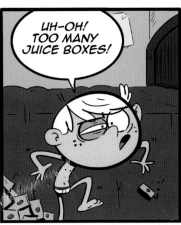

READING COMICS ALL AFTERNOON -- THE PERFECT SATURDAY!
UH-OH! TOO MANY JUICE BOXES!

the episode "Undie Pressure," it's revealed that Lincoln Loud enjoys reading his comics wearing only his derpants, much to the dismay of his sisters. That got us to thinking about how people read their comics d graphic novels.

f Whitman, editor of *THE LOUD HOUSE* graphic novels, enjoys reading comics on a couch, on his ur-long subway ride home, and in the park, where it's particularly peaceful.

ichelle Hart, our Marketing Coordinator, tends to get her comics digitally. She especially enjoys being ole to enlarge comics lettering on her screen for her sore eyes. Her favorite places to read comics are her in bed or on the back porch.

hen I was a kid, I read comics in bed too. I would lay tummy-down on my old iron folding bed with my ad hanging out over the top and my mouth resting on part of the flat metal bedframe, while the comic as on the floor or in my hands. This actually pushed back my front teeth—it was as if I wore braces to ake my teeth crooked!

en there's how we keep our comics once we're done reading them. Lincoln wants to keep his prized omics in perfect condition, and goes to great lengths to preserve his comic in "Bagged and Boarded," ly to be ultimately frustrated. I can relate! Other kids might just roll up their comics and keep them in eir back pockets. What do you like to do with yours?

owever you like to read and keep your comics, the important thing is that you enjoy them, especially those blished by Papercutz, such as *BREADWINNERS*, *HARVEY BEAKS*, *NICKELODEON PANDEMONIUM!*, *G GOAT BANANA CRICKET* (check out the preview on the following pages!), and of course, *THE LOUD OUSE!* Don't miss Volume 3, coming soon—and feel free to enjoy it any way you like!

THE HERO

Thanks,

Jim

STAY IN TOUCH!

EMAIL:	salicrup@papercutz.com
WEB:	papercutz.com
TWITTER:	@papercutzgn
INSTAGRAM:	@papercutzgn
FACEBOOK:	PAPERCUTZGRAPHICNOVELS
FANMAIL:	Papercutz, 160 Broadway, Suite 700, East Wing, New York, NY 10038

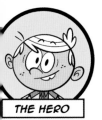

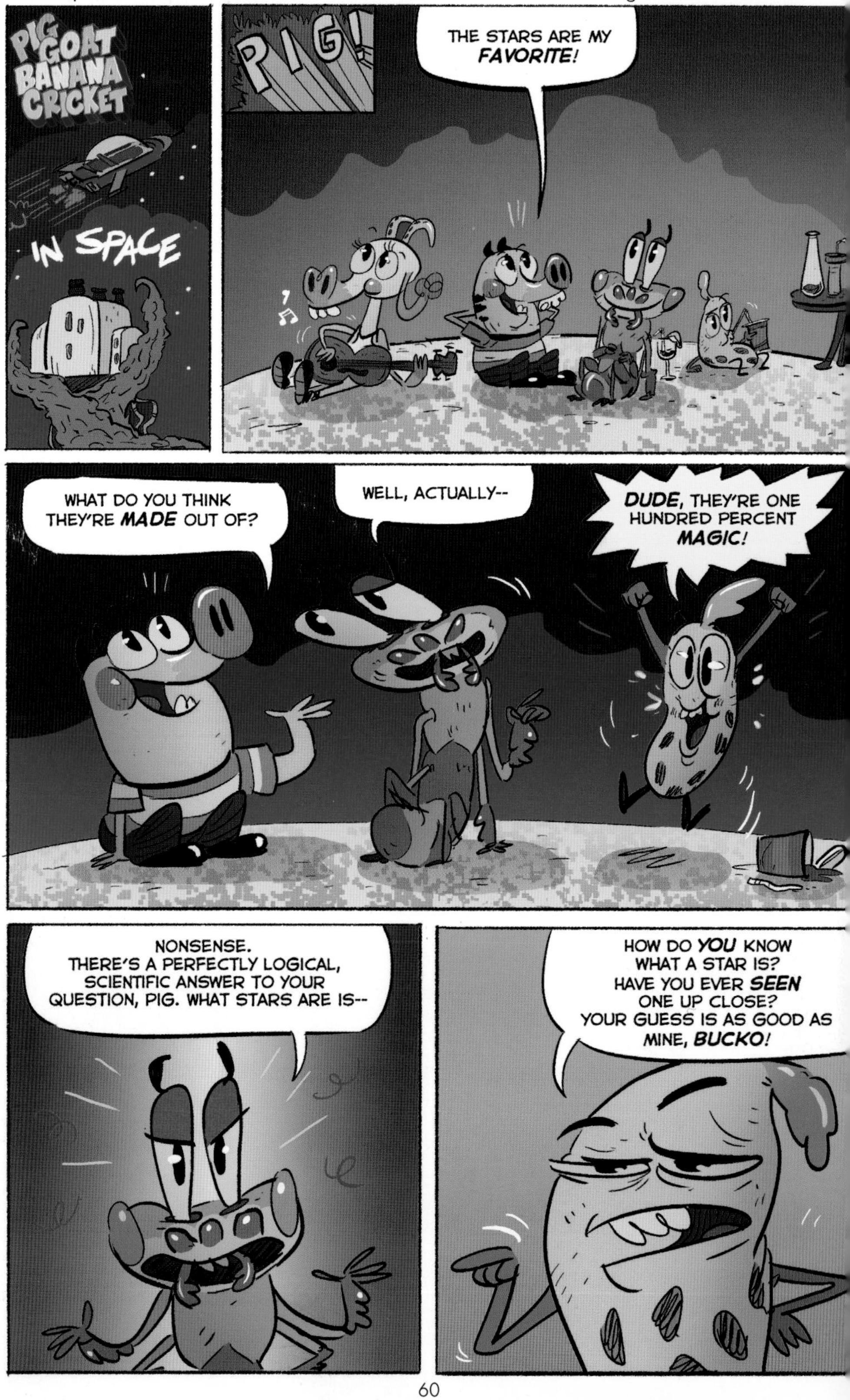
PIG GOAT BANANA CRICKET
IN SPACE
PIG!
THE STARS ARE MY FAVORITE!
WHAT DO YOU THINK THEY'RE MADE OUT OF?
WELL, ACTUALLY--
DUDE, THEY'RE ONE HUNDRED PERCENT MAGIC!
NONSENSE. THERE'S A PERFECTLY LOGICAL, SCIENTIFIC ANSWER TO YOUR QUESTION, PIG. WHAT STARS ARE IS--
HOW DO YOU KNOW WHAT A STAR IS? HAVE YOU EVER SEEN ONE UP CLOSE? YOUR GUESS IS AS GOOD AS MINE, BUCKO!

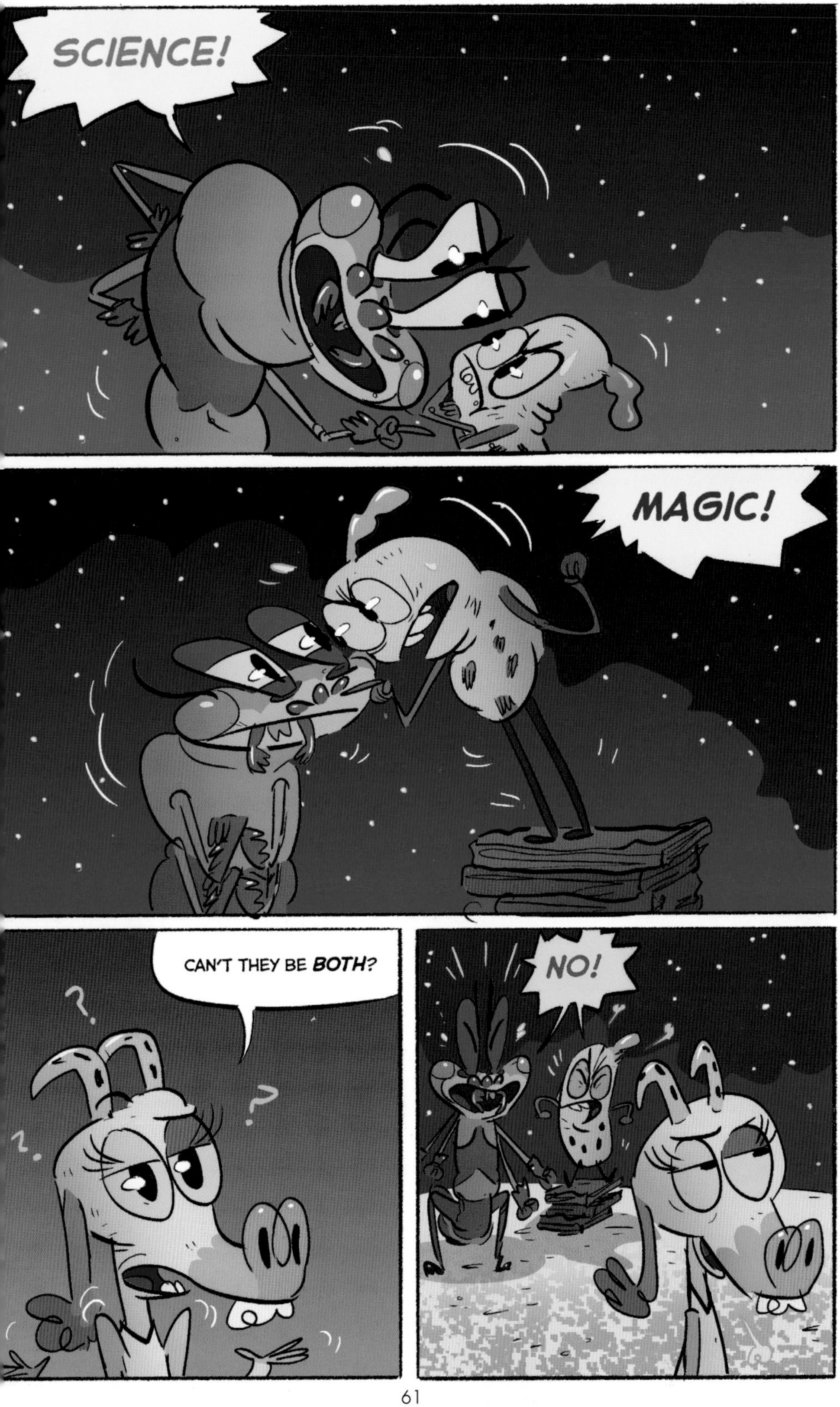

SCIENCE!
MAGIC!
CAN'T THEY BE *BOTH*?
NO!

PIG, STARS ARE *EXPLODING* BALLS OF GAS THAT ARE HELD TOGETHER BY THEIR OWN GRAVITY! THAT ONE IS CALLED *ALNILAM*, AND IT IS 375,000 TIMES BRIGHTER THAN *THE SUN!*

WHOA! THAT'S *AWESOME!*

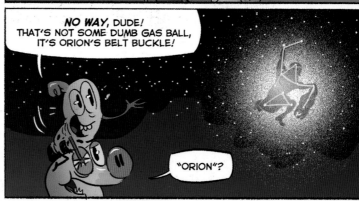

NO WAY, DUDE! THAT'S NOT SOME DUMB GAS BALL, IT'S ORION'S BELT BUCKLE!

"ORION"?

YEAH, DUDE! HE'S THIS ANCIENT GREEK *SUPERHERO* WHO COULD WALK ON WATER AND HAD THE POWER TO *TAME* ANY BEAST. HE *RULED* SO HARD, ZEUS TURNED HIM INTO STARS WHEN HE KICKED THE BUCKET.

THAT'S RIDICULOUS!

IF YOU'RE SO SURE IT'S NOT ORION, THEN WHY DON'T YOU GO PROVE IT?

MAYBE. I. WILL!

OH, BROTHER.

To be concluded in NICKELODEON PANDEMONIUM! #3!

OR
ORE

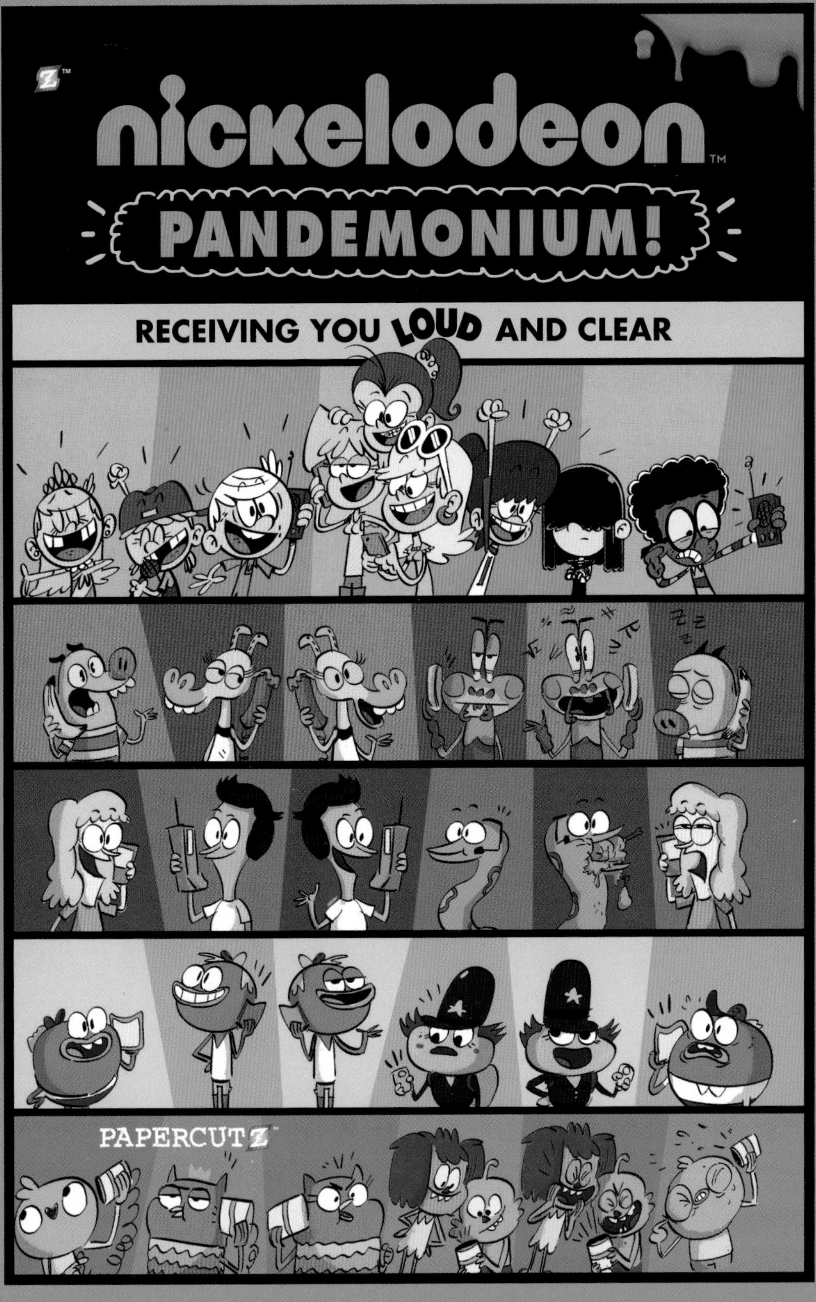
nickelodeon
PANDEMONIUM!
RECEIVING YOU LOUD AND CLEAR
PAPERCUTZ

**CHECK OUT NICKELODEON PANDEMONIUM! #3
ON SALE NOW!**

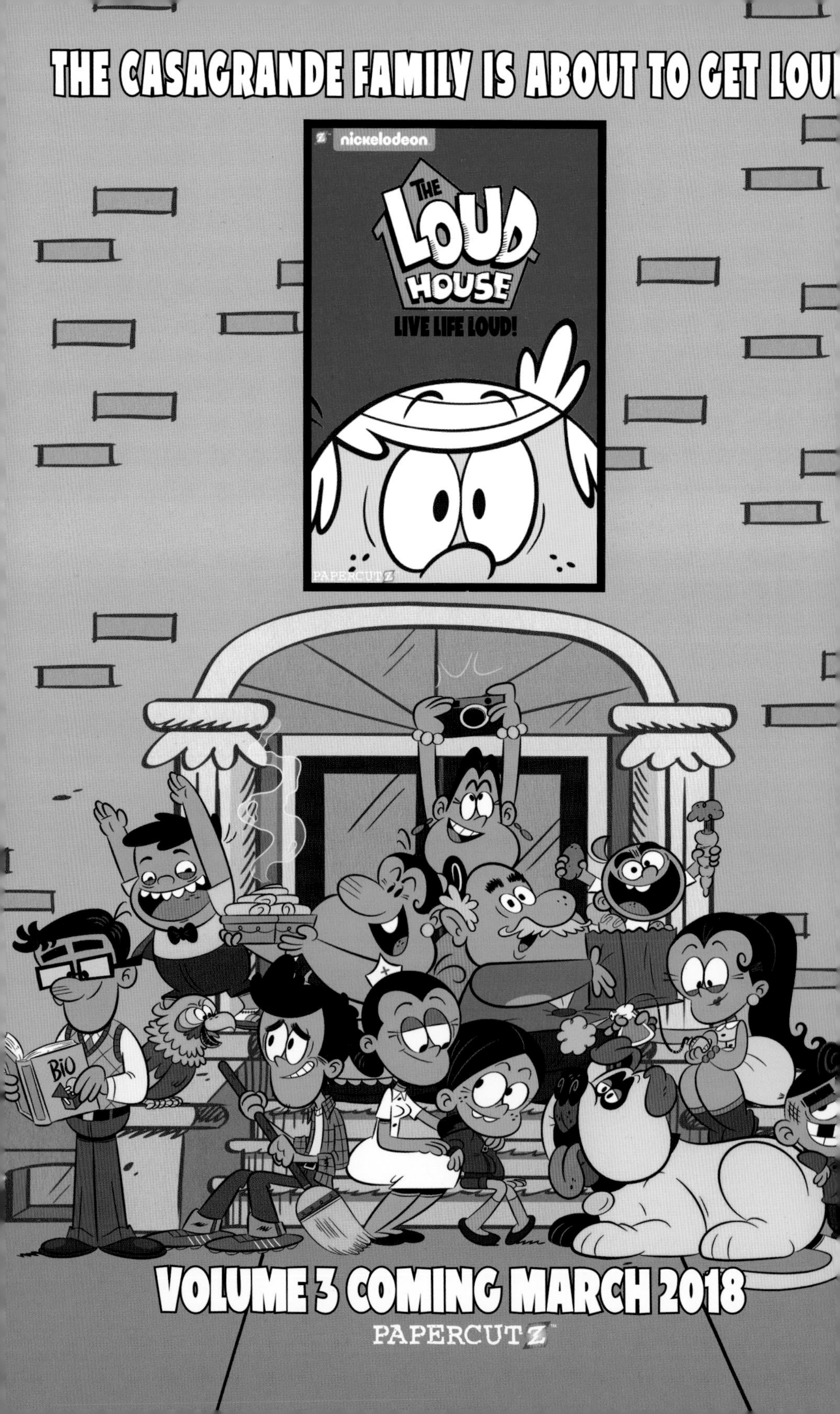
THE CASAGRANDE FAMILY IS ABOUT TO GET LOU
nickelodeon
THE LOUD HOUSE
LIVE LIFE LOUD!
PAPERCUTZ
BIO
VOLUME 3 COMING MARCH 2018
PAPERCUTZ

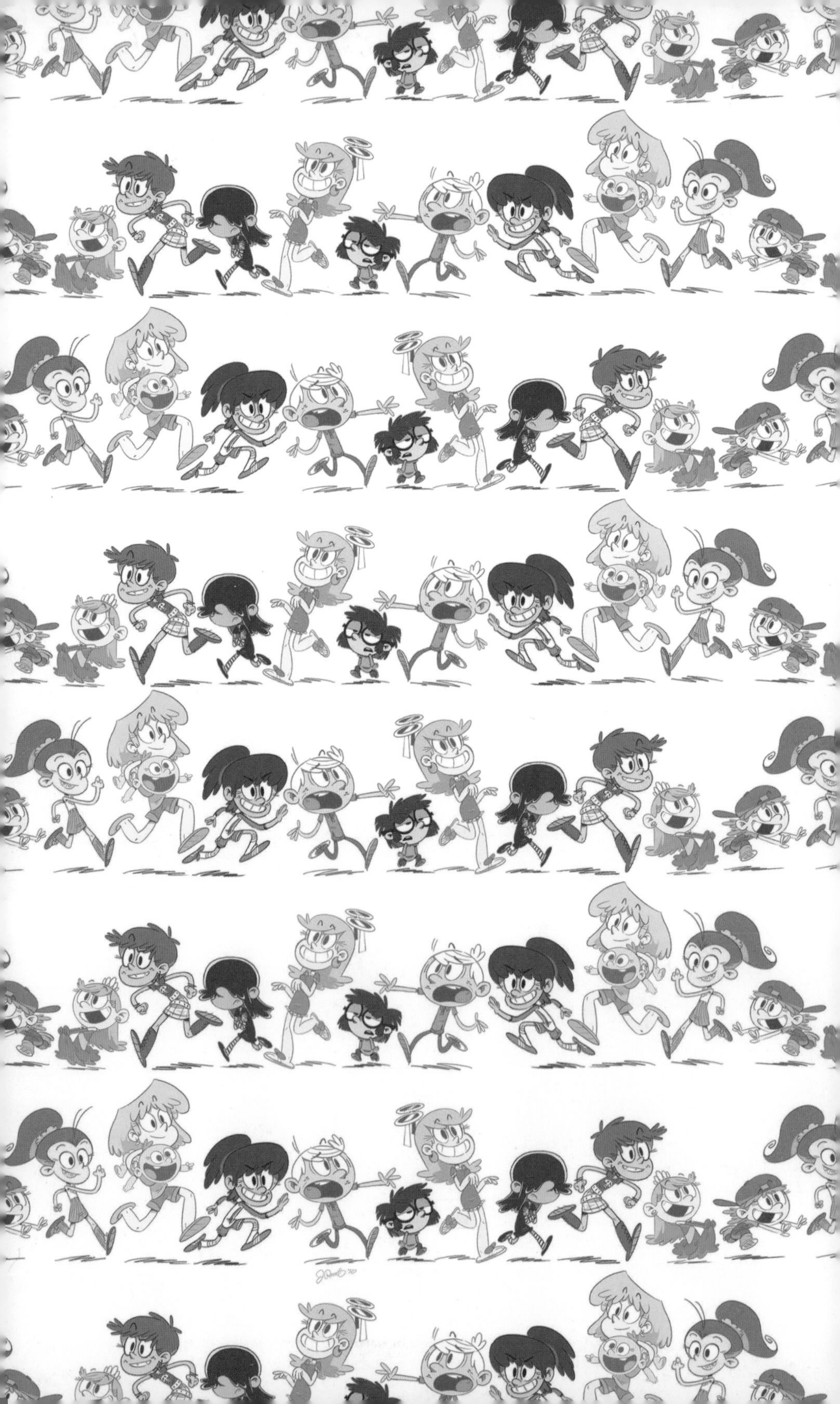